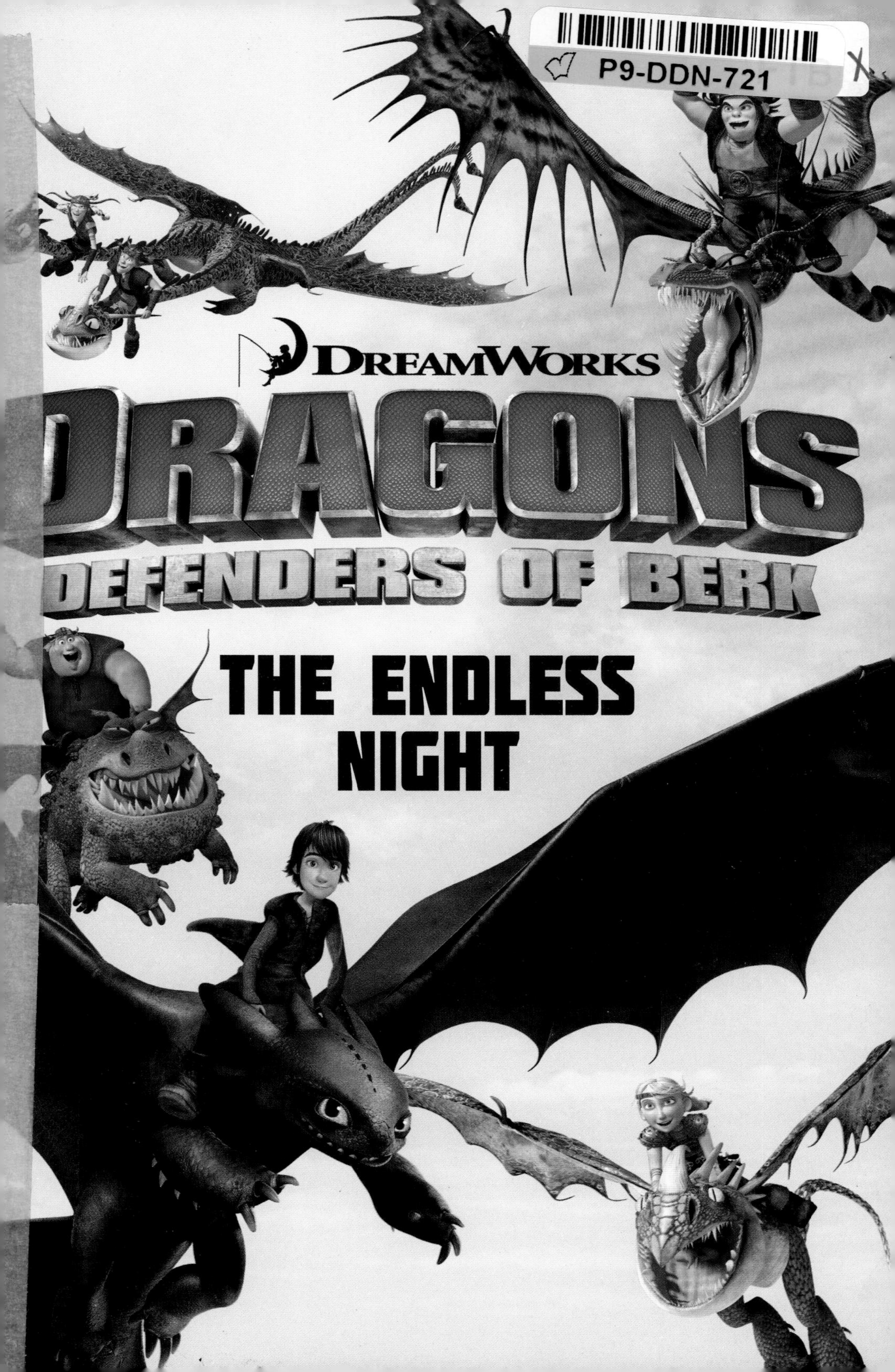
DreamWorks
DRAGONS
DEFENDERS OF BERK
THE ENDLESS NIGHT

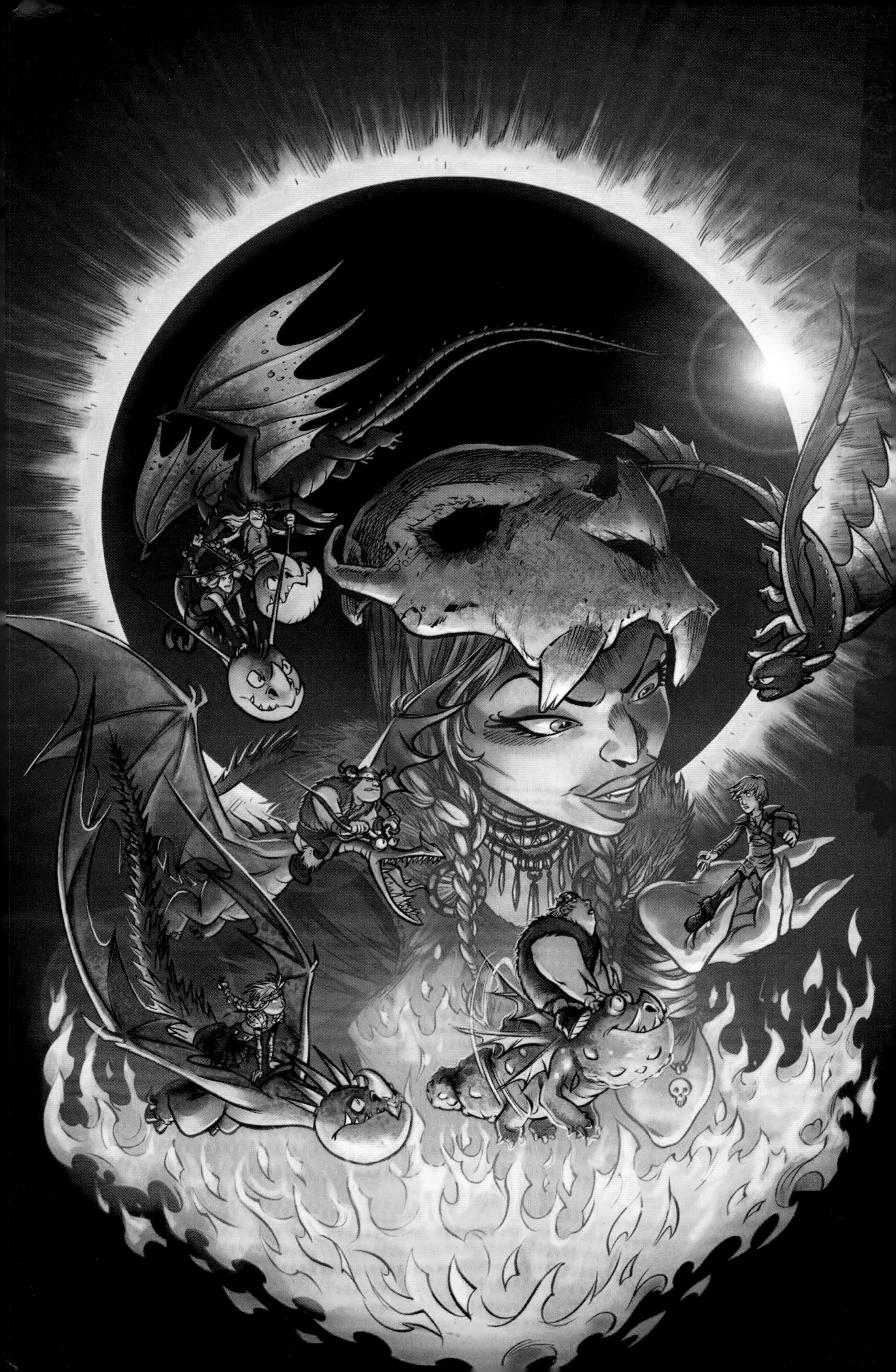

GRAPHIC NOVEL J F FUR
1873 0492 12-06-2016 FTB
Furman, Simon,

Dragons, defenders of Berk.
KHP

DREAMWORKS

DRAGONS
DEFENDERS OF BERK

THE ENDLESS NIGHT

SCRIPT
SIMON FURMAN

PENCILS
IWAN NAZIF

COLORS
DIGIKORE

LETTERING
JIM CAMPBELL

TITAN
COMICS

DREAMWORKS

DRAGONS

DEFENDERS OF BERK

Welcome to Berk, the home of Hiccup and his dragon, Toothless, plus Hiccup's friends who train at the Dragon Training Academy!

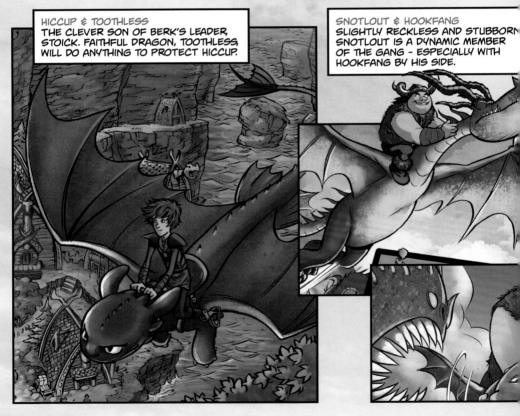

HICCUP & TOOTHLESS
THE CLEVER SON OF BERK'S LEADER, STOICK. FAITHFUL DRAGON, TOOTHLESS, WILL DO ANYTHING TO PROTECT HICCUP.

SNOTLOUT & HOOKFANG
SLIGHTLY RECKLESS AND STUBBORN, SNOTLOUT IS A DYNAMIC MEMBER OF THE GANG - ESPECIALLY WITH HOOKFANG BY HIS SIDE.

TITAN COMICS

Senior Editor
MARTIN EDEN
Production Manager
OBI ONOURA
Production Supervisors
MARIA PEARSON,
JACKIE FLOOK

Production Assistant
PETER JAMES
Studio Manager
SELINA JUNEJA
Senior Sales Manager
STEVE TOTHILL

Marketing Manager
RICKY CLAYDON
Publishing Manager
DARRYL TOTHILL
Publishing Director
CHRIS TEATHER

Operations Director
LEIGH BAULCH
Executive Director
VIVIAN CHEUNG
Publisher
NICK LANDAU

RUFFNUT & TUFFNUT/BARF & BELCH
THESE TROUBLESOME TWINS AND THEIR TWO-HEADED DRAGON MAKE FOR A DOUBLY POWERFUL FORCE.

GOBBER
A LONG-TIME FRIEND AND ADVISOR OF STOICK.

STOICK THE VAST
THE TOUGH CHIEF OF BERK, AND HICCUP'S DEMANDING FATHER.

FISHLEGS & MEATLUG
A DRAGON EXPERT WITH A HEART OF GOLD — AND HIS TRUSTED FRIEND!

ASTRID & STORMFLY
A STRONG WARRIOR WITH HER TRUSTY AXE — AND LOYAL DRAGON — BY HER SIDE!

ISBN: 9781782762140
DreamWorks Dragons: Defenders of Berk: The Endless Night, published by Titan Comics, a division of Titan Publishing Group Ltd.
144 Southwark St. London, SE1 0UP

DreamWorks Dragons: Defenders of Berk © 2016 DreamWorks Animation LLC. All Rights Reserved. No part of this publication may be reproduced, stored in a retrieval system, or transmitted, in any form or by any means, without the prior written permission of the publisher. Names, characters, places and incidents featured in this publication are either the product of the author's imagination or used fictitiously. Any resemblance to actual persons, living or dead (except for satirical purposes), is entirely coincidental.

10 9 8 7 6 5 4 3 2 1
First printed in China in February 2016.
A CIP catalogue record for this title is available from the British Library.
Titan Comics. TC0518
Special thanks to Corinne Combs, Barbara Layman, Lawrence Hamashima, & all at DreamWorks. Also, Andre Siregar and Elitsa Veshkova.

CHAPTER ONE

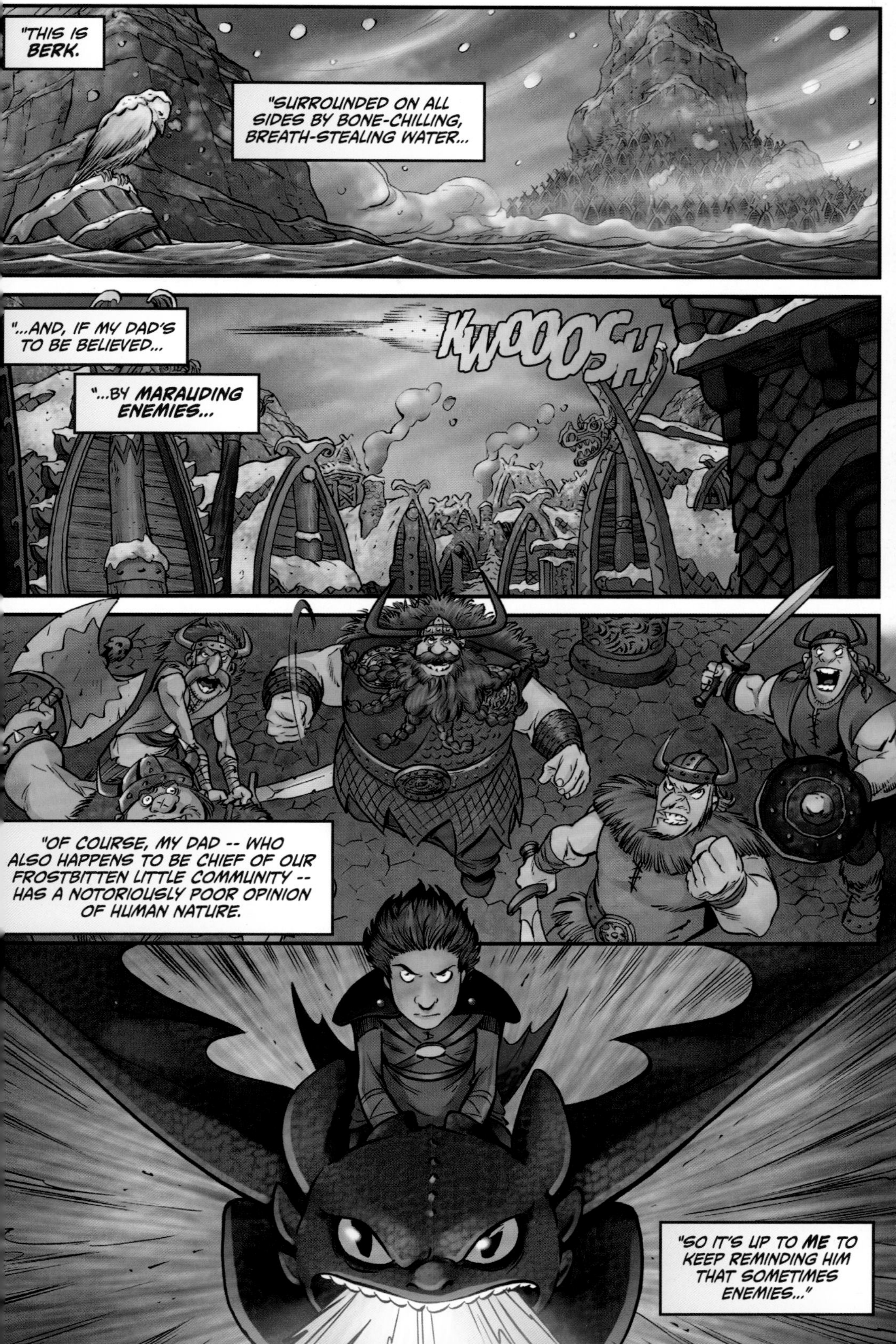
"THIS IS BERK.
"SURROUNDED ON ALL SIDES BY BONE-CHILLING, BREATH-STEALING WATER...
"...AND, IF MY DAD'S TO BE BELIEVED...
"...BY MARAUDING ENEMIES...
KWOOOSH
"OF COURSE, MY DAD -- WHO ALSO HAPPENS TO BE CHIEF OF OUR FROSTBITTEN LITTLE COMMUNITY -- HAS A NOTORIOUSLY POOR OPINION OF HUMAN NATURE.
"SO IT'S UP TO ME TO KEEP REMINDING HIM THAT SOMETIMES ENEMIES..."

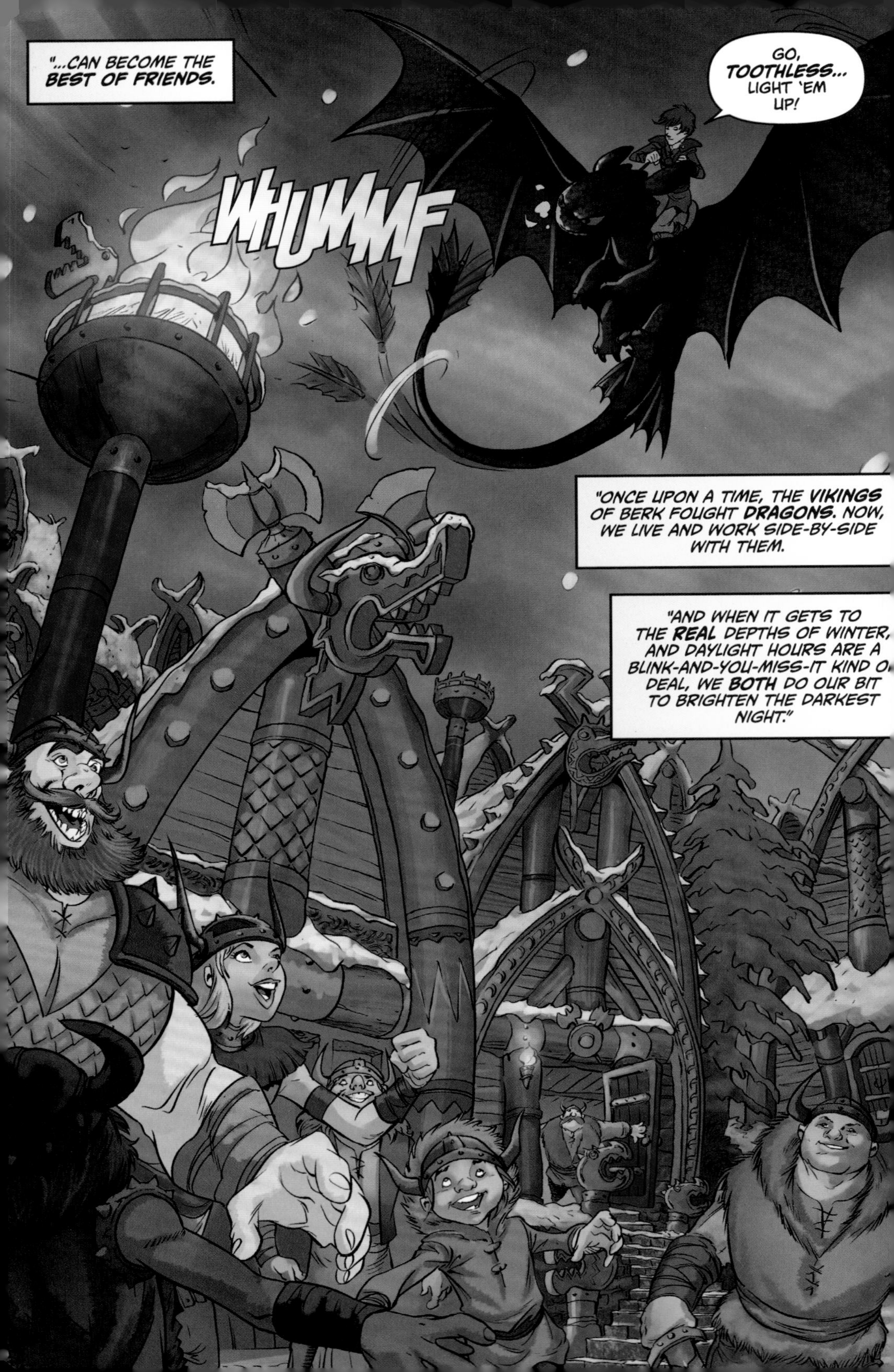
"...CAN BECOME THE BEST OF FRIENDS.
GO, TOOTHLESS... LIGHT 'EM UP!
WHUMMF
"ONCE UPON A TIME, THE VIKINGS OF BERK FOUGHT DRAGONS. NOW, WE LIVE AND WORK SIDE-BY-SIDE WITH THEM.
"AND WHEN IT GETS TO THE REAL DEPTHS OF WINTER, AND DAYLIGHT HOURS ARE A BLINK-AND-YOU-MISS-IT KIND OF DEAL, WE BOTH DO OUR BIT TO BRIGHTEN THE DARKEST NIGHT."

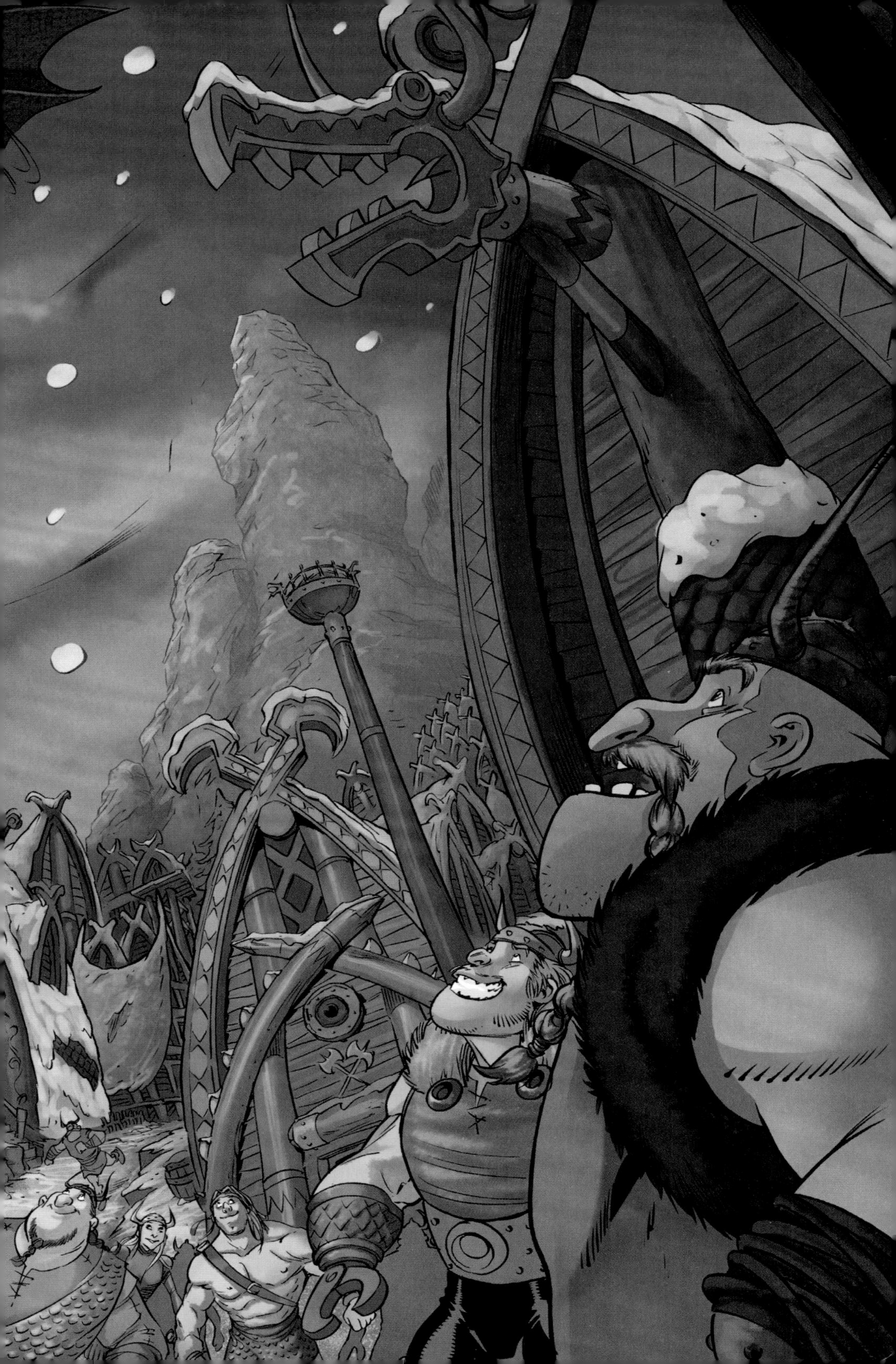

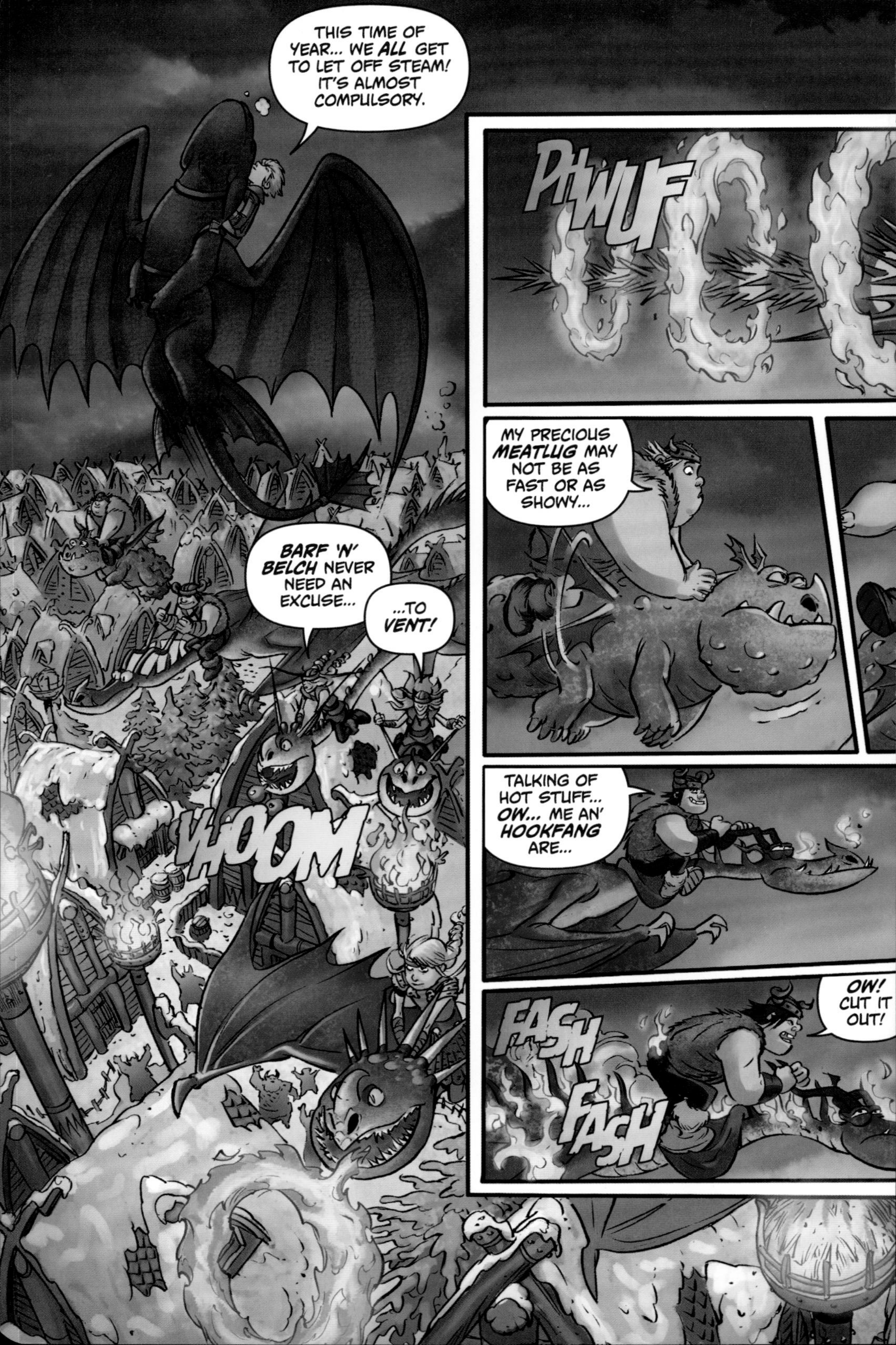
THIS TIME OF YEAR... WE ALL GET TO LET OFF STEAM! IT'S ALMOST COMPULSORY.
BARF 'N' BELCH NEVER NEED AN EXCUSE...
...TO VENT!
VHOOM
PHWUF
MY PRECIOUS MEATLUG MAY NOT BE AS FAST OR AS SHOWY...
TALKING OF HOT STUFF... OW... ME AN' HOOKFANG ARE...
FASH
FASH
OW! CUT IT OUT!

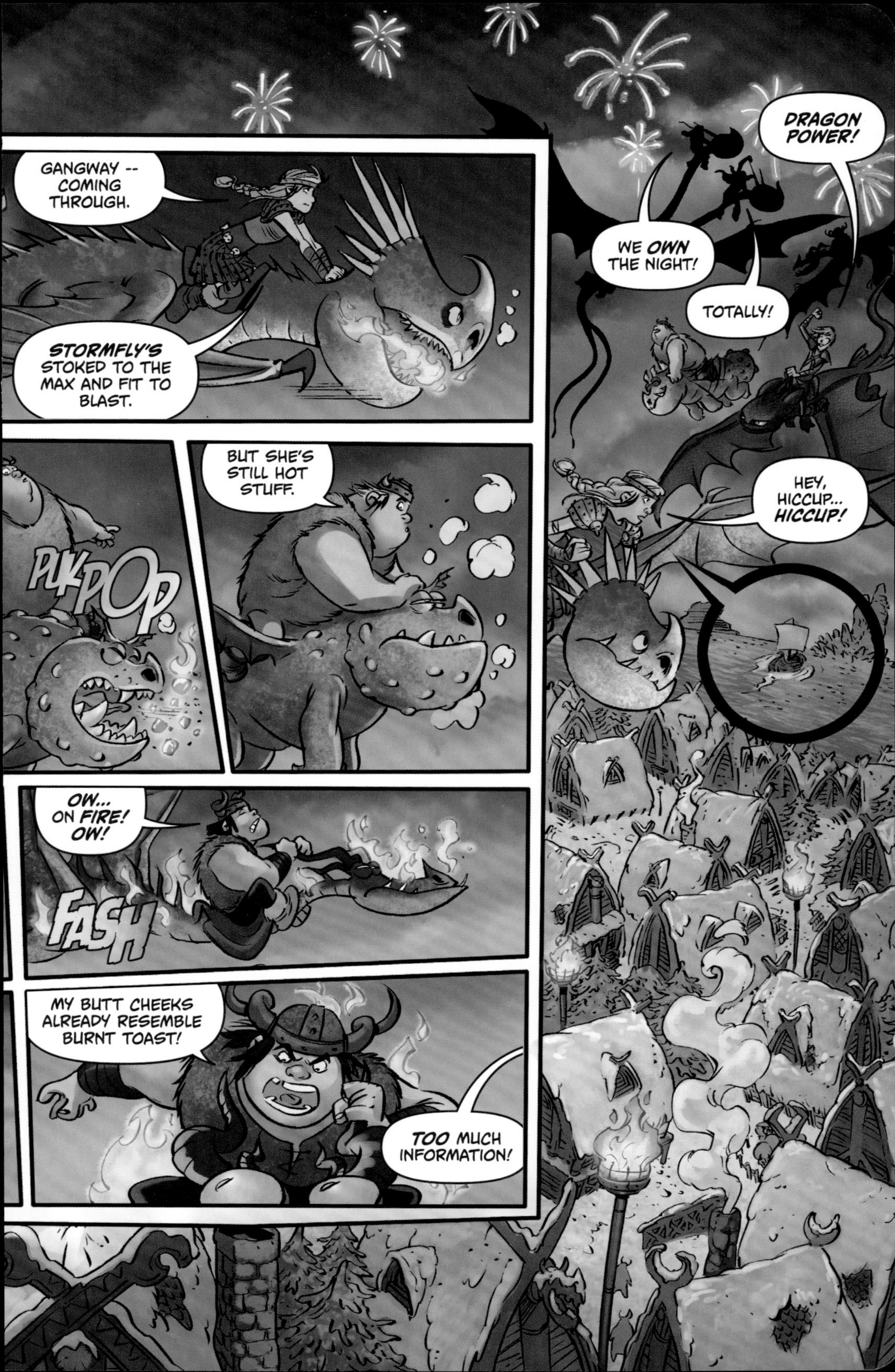
GANGWAY -- COMING THROUGH.
STORMFLY'S STOKED TO THE MAX AND FIT TO BLAST.
DRAGON POWER!
WE OWN THE NIGHT!
TOTALLY!
PUK POP
BUT SHE'S STILL HOT STUFF.
HEY, HICCUP... HICCUP!
OW... ON FIRE! OW!
FASH
MY BUTT CHEEKS ALREADY RESEMBLE BURNT TOAST!
TOO MUCH INFORMATION!

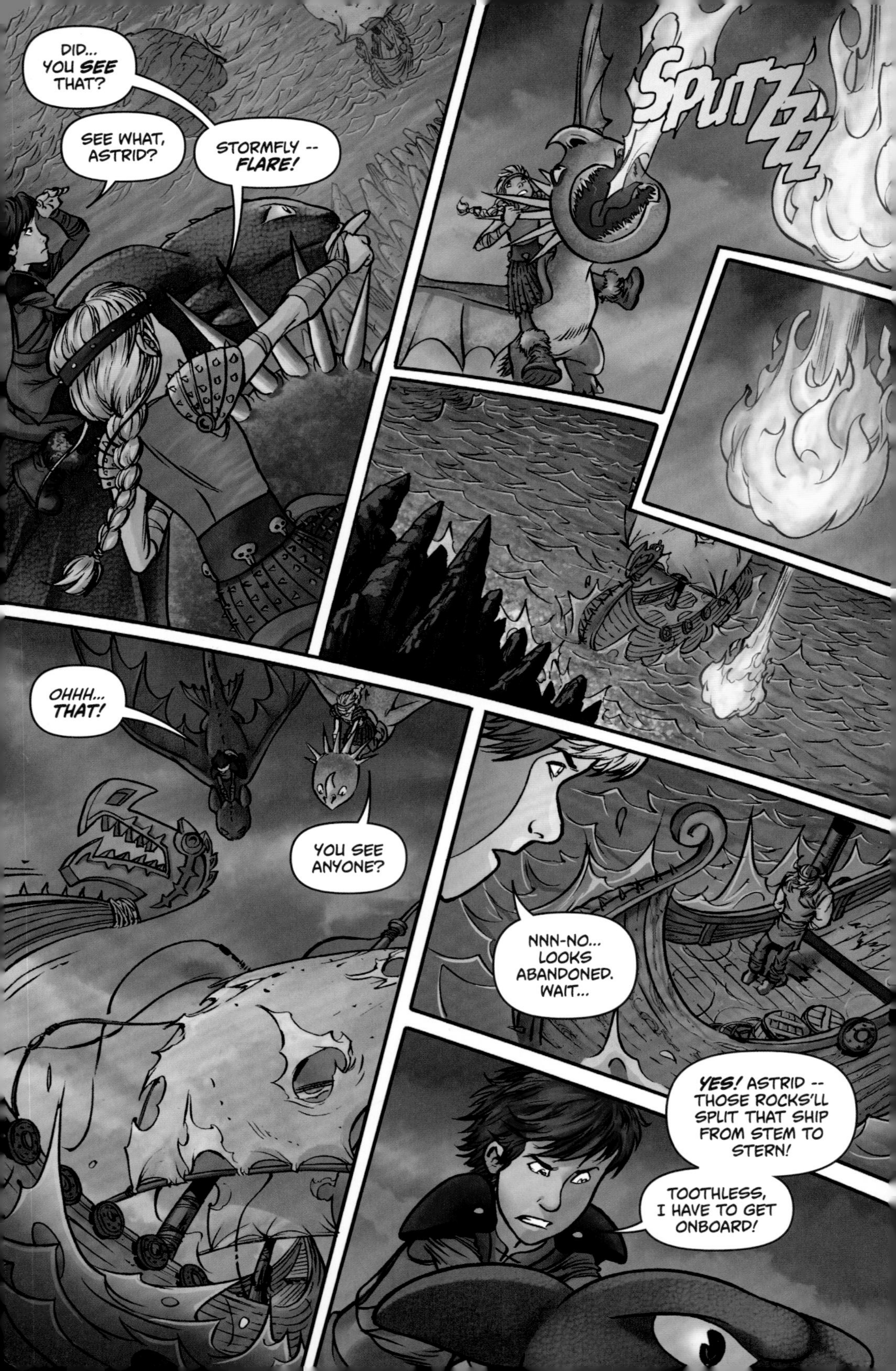

DID... YOU **SEE** THAT?
SEE WHAT, ASTRID?
STORMFLY -- **FLARE!**
SPUTZZZ
OHHH... **THAT!**
YOU SEE ANYONE?
NNN-NO... LOOKS ABANDONED. WAIT...
YES! ASTRID -- THOSE ROCKS'LL SPLIT THAT SHIP FROM STEM TO STERN!
TOOTHLESS, I HAVE TO GET ONBOARD!

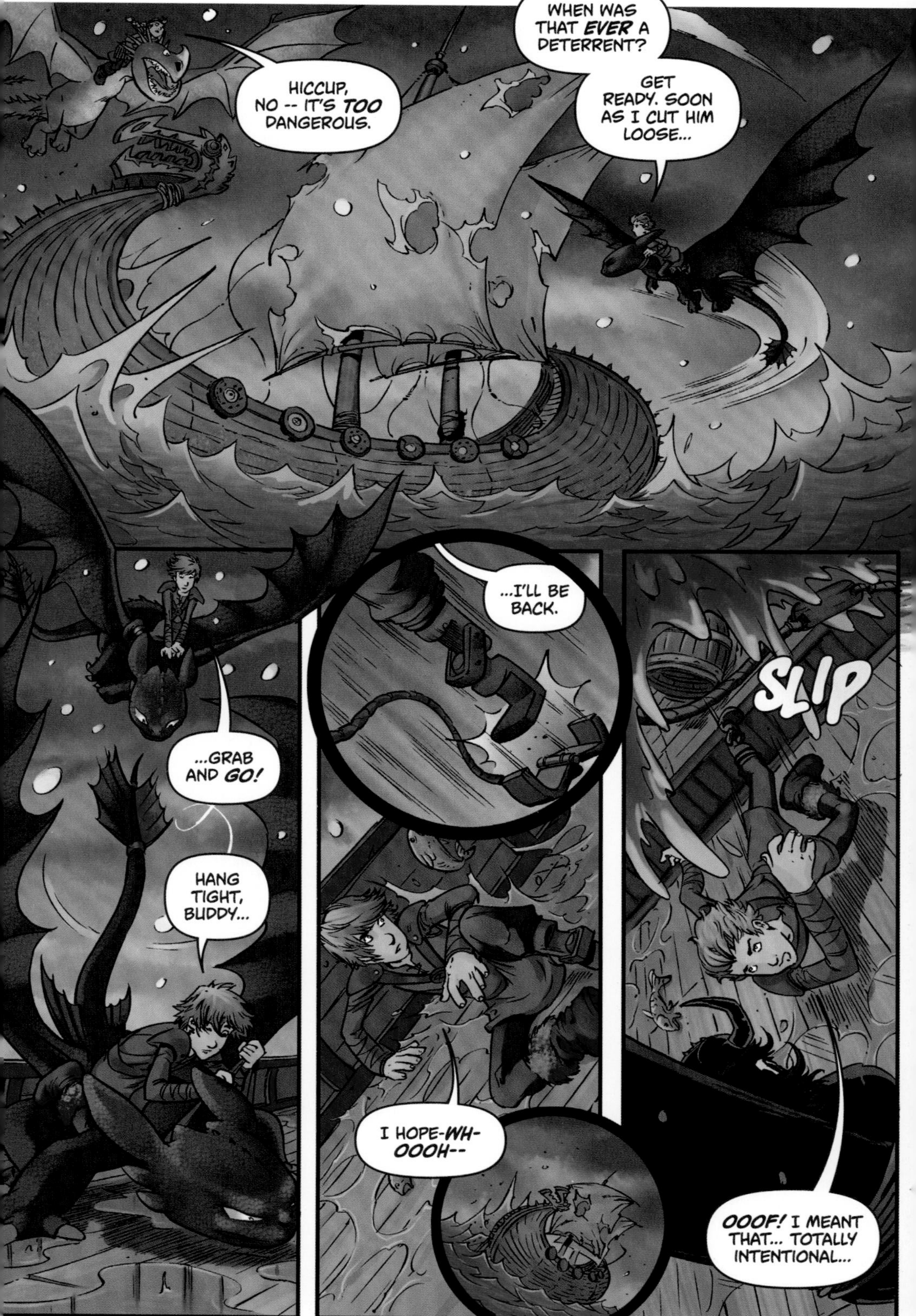
HICCUP, NO -- IT'S *TOO* DANGEROUS.
WHEN WAS THAT *EVER* A DETERRENT?
GET READY. SOON AS I CUT HIM LOOSE...
...GRAB AND *GO!*
HANG TIGHT, BUDDY...
...I'LL BE BACK.
I HOPE-*WH-OOOH--*
SLIP
OOOF! I MEANT THAT... TOTALLY INTENTIONAL...

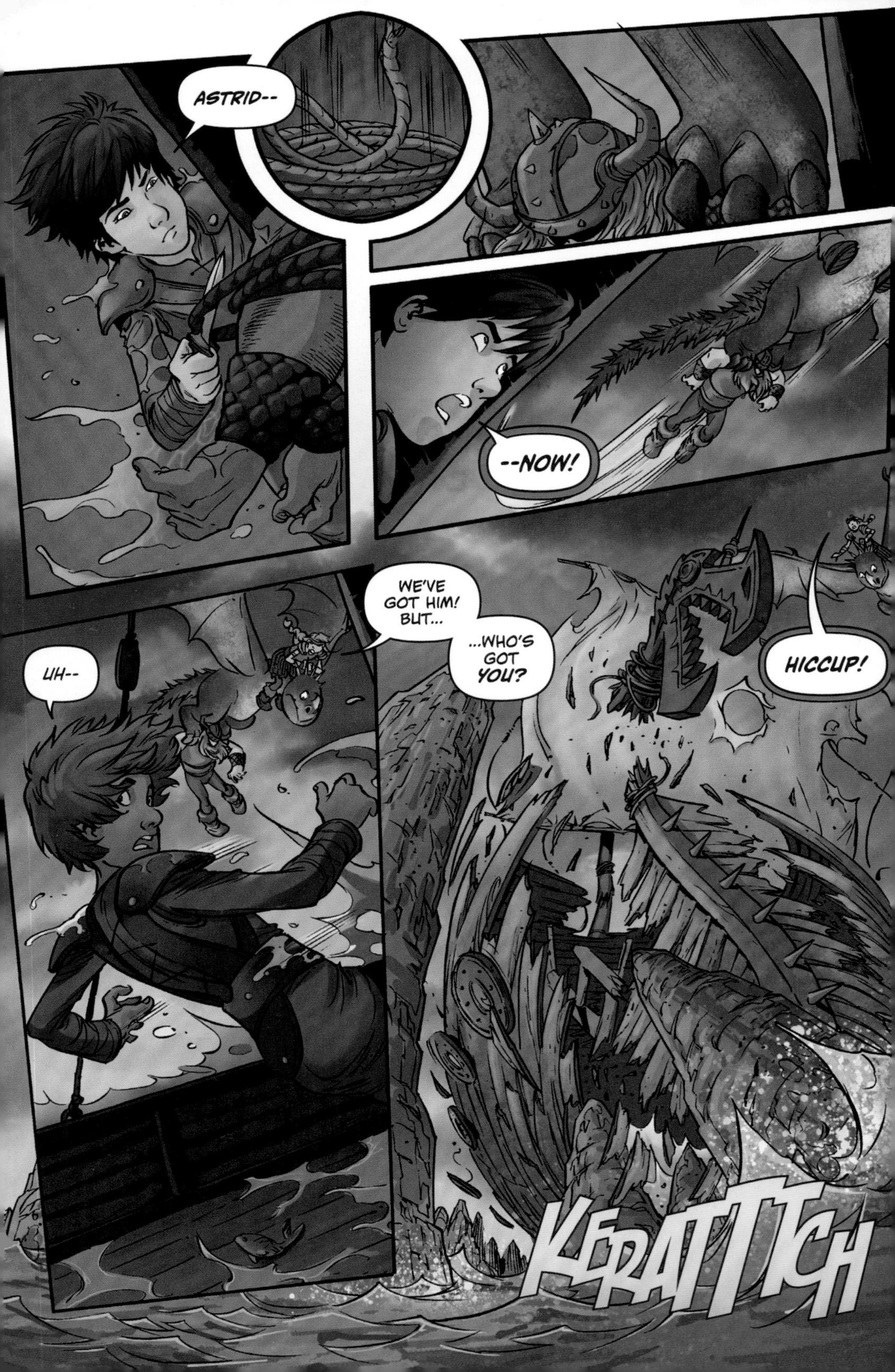
ASTRID--
--NOW!
UH--
WE'VE GOT HIM! BUT...
...WHO'S GOT YOU?
HICCUP!
KERATTTCH

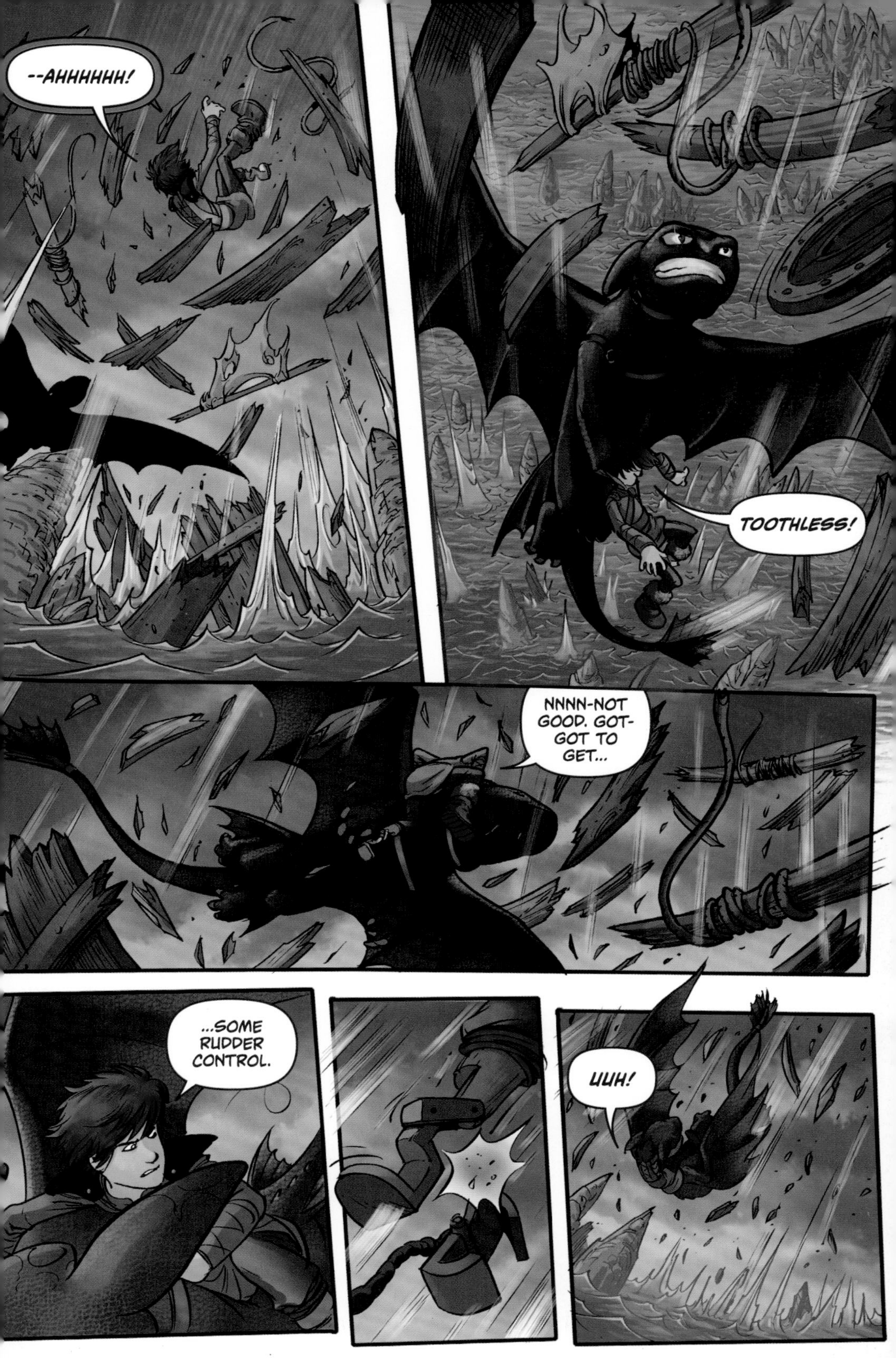
--AHHHHHH!
TOOTHLESS!
NNNN-NOT GOOD. GOT-GOT TO GET...
...SOME RUDDER CONTROL.
UUH!

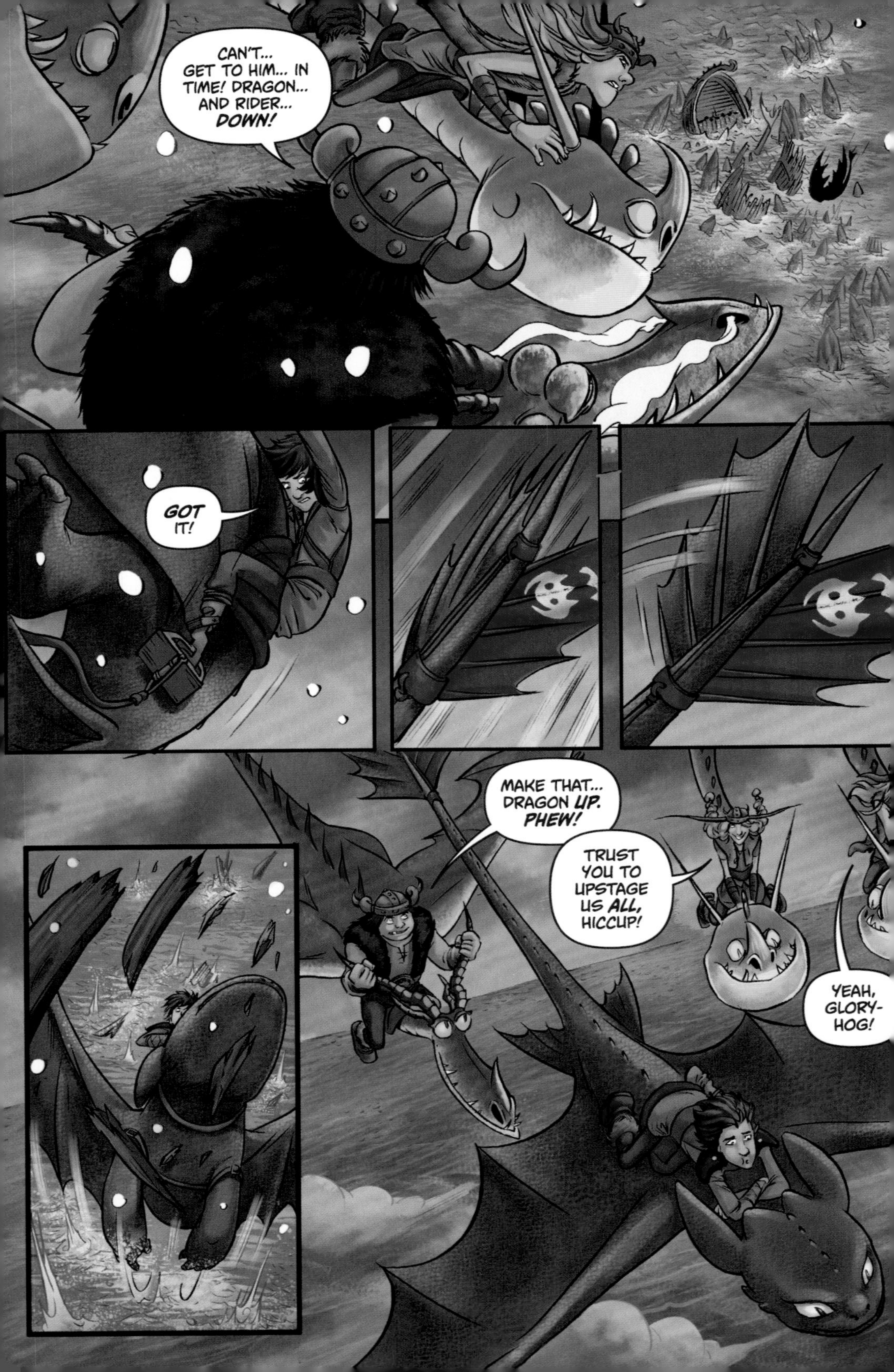

CAN'T... GET TO HIM... IN TIME! DRAGON... AND RIDER... DOWN!
GOT IT!
MAKE THAT... DRAGON UP. PHEW!
TRUST YOU TO UPSTAGE US ALL, HICCUP!
YEAH, GLORY-HOG!

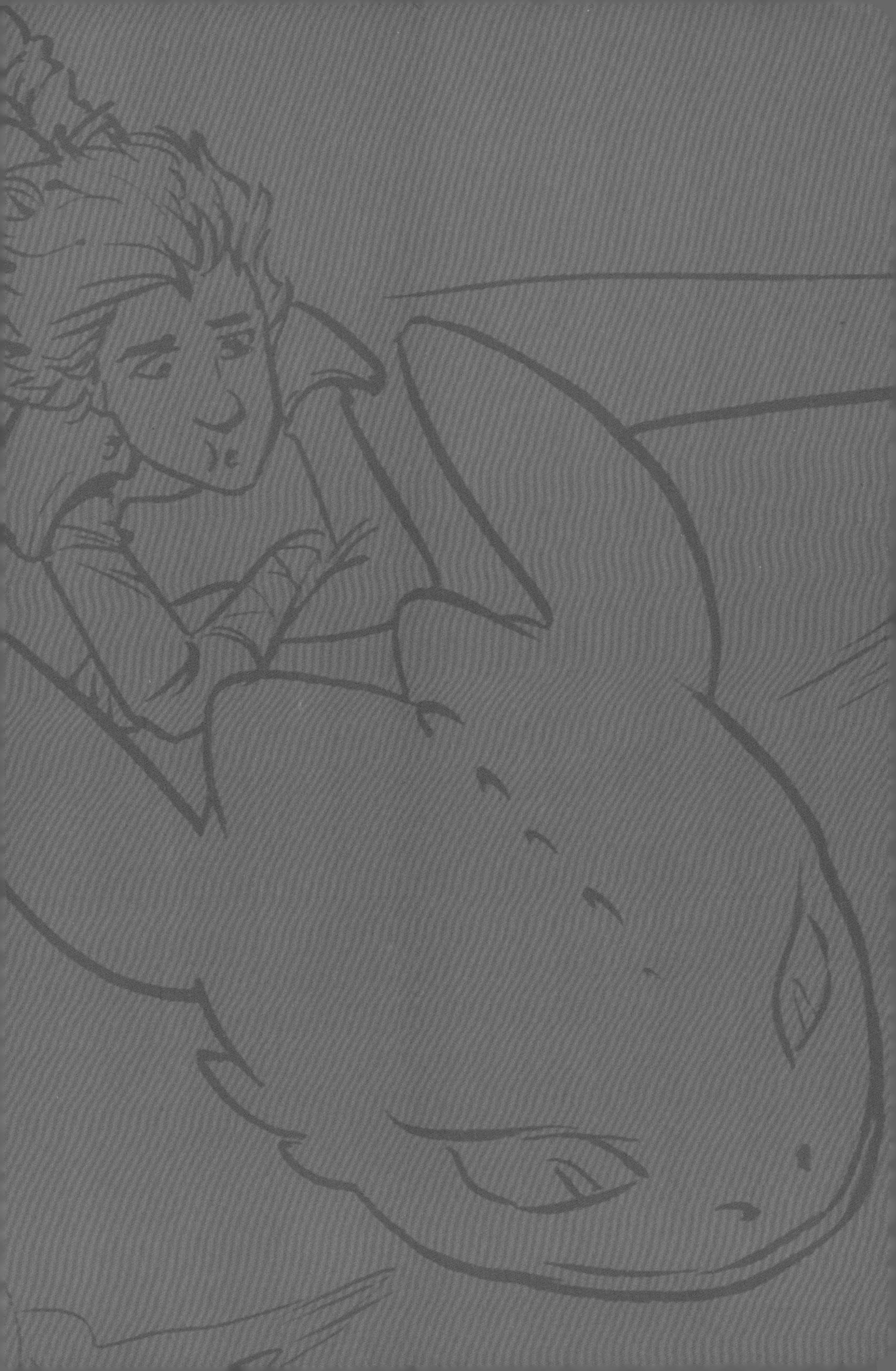

CHAPTER TWO

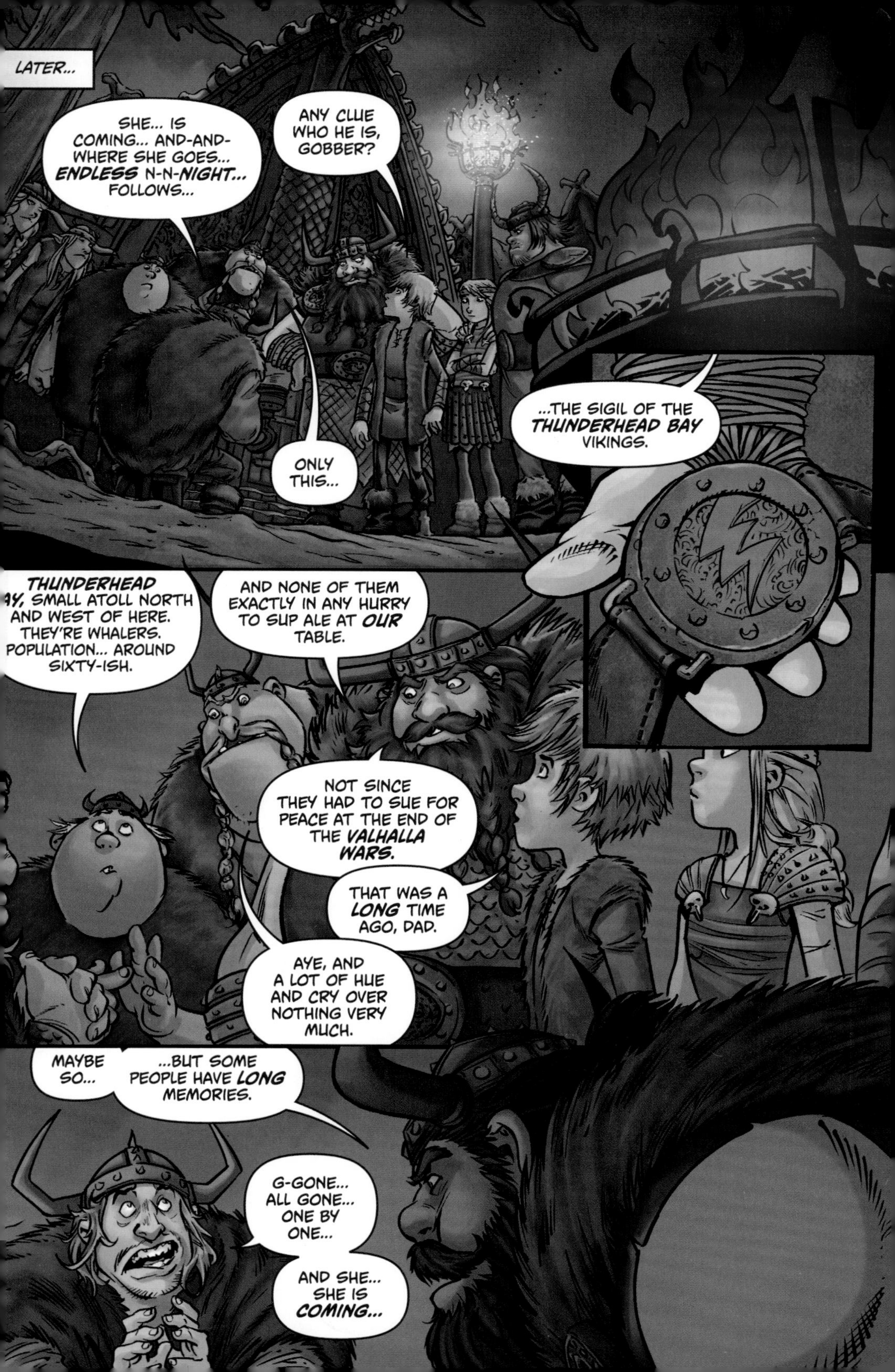
LATER...
SHE... IS COMING... AND-AND- WHERE SHE GOES... ENDLESS N-N-NIGHT... FOLLOWS...
ANY CLUE WHO HE IS, GOBBER?
ONLY THIS...
...THE SIGIL OF THE THUNDERHEAD BAY VIKINGS.
THUNDERHEAD BAY, SMALL ATOLL NORTH AND WEST OF HERE. THEY'RE WHALERS. POPULATION... AROUND SIXTY-ISH.
AND NONE OF THEM EXACTLY IN ANY HURRY TO SUP ALE AT OUR TABLE.
NOT SINCE THEY HAD TO SUE FOR PEACE AT THE END OF THE VALHALLA WARS.
THAT WAS A LONG TIME AGO, DAD.
AYE, AND A LOT OF HUE AND CRY OVER NOTHING VERY MUCH.
MAYBE SO...
...BUT SOME PEOPLE HAVE LONG MEMORIES.
G-GONE... ALL GONE... ONE BY ONE...
AND SHE... SHE IS COMING...

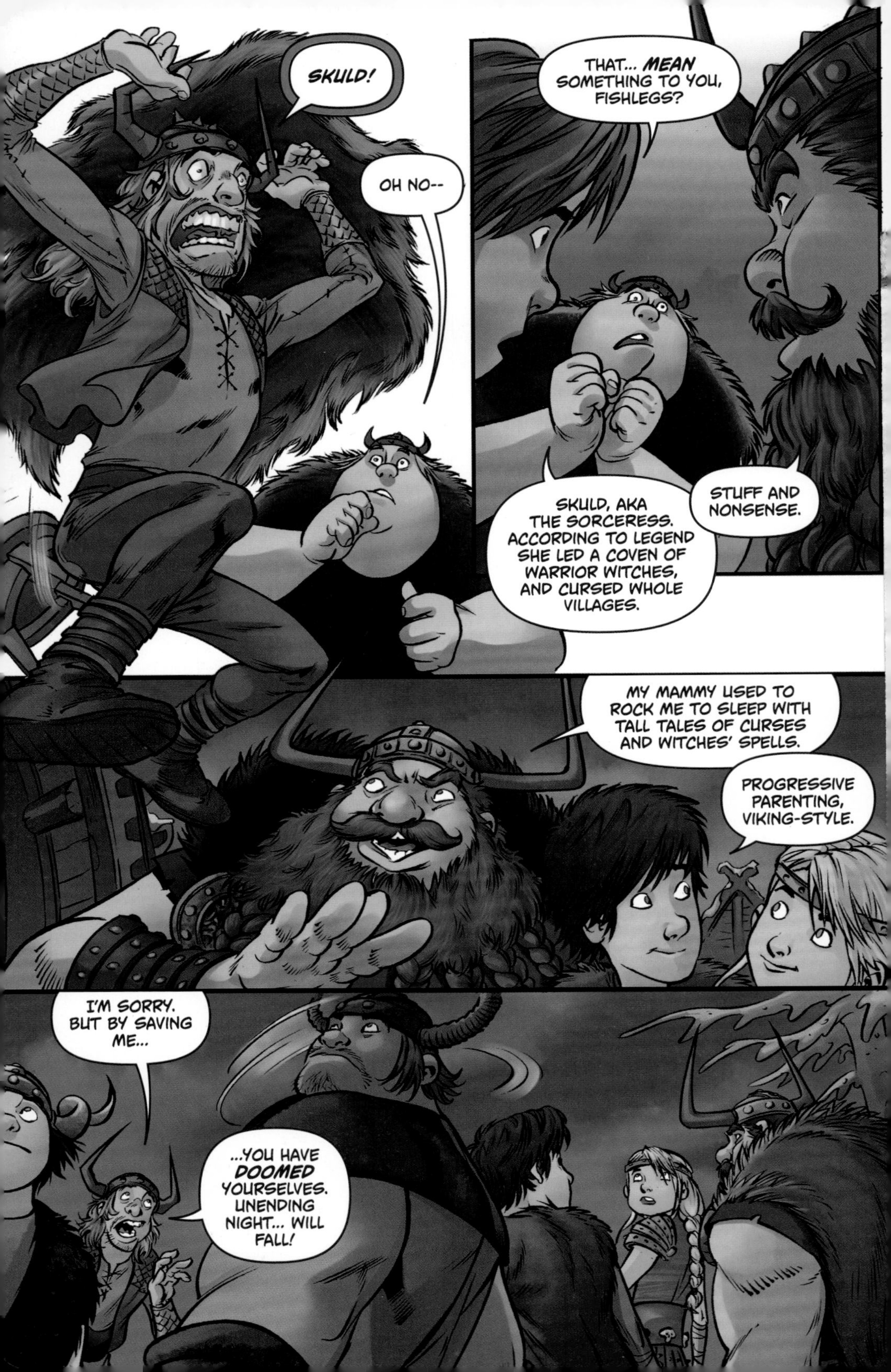
SKULD!
OH NO--
THAT... MEAN SOMETHING TO YOU, FISHLEGS?
SKULD, AKA THE SORCERESS. ACCORDING TO LEGEND SHE LED A COVEN OF WARRIOR WITCHES, AND CURSED WHOLE VILLAGES.
STUFF AND NONSENSE.
MY MAMMY USED TO ROCK ME TO SLEEP WITH TALL TALES OF CURSES AND WITCHES' SPELLS.
PROGRESSIVE PARENTING, VIKING-STYLE.
I'M SORRY. BUT BY SAVING ME...
...YOU HAVE DOOMED YOURSELVES. UNENDING NIGHT... WILL FALL!

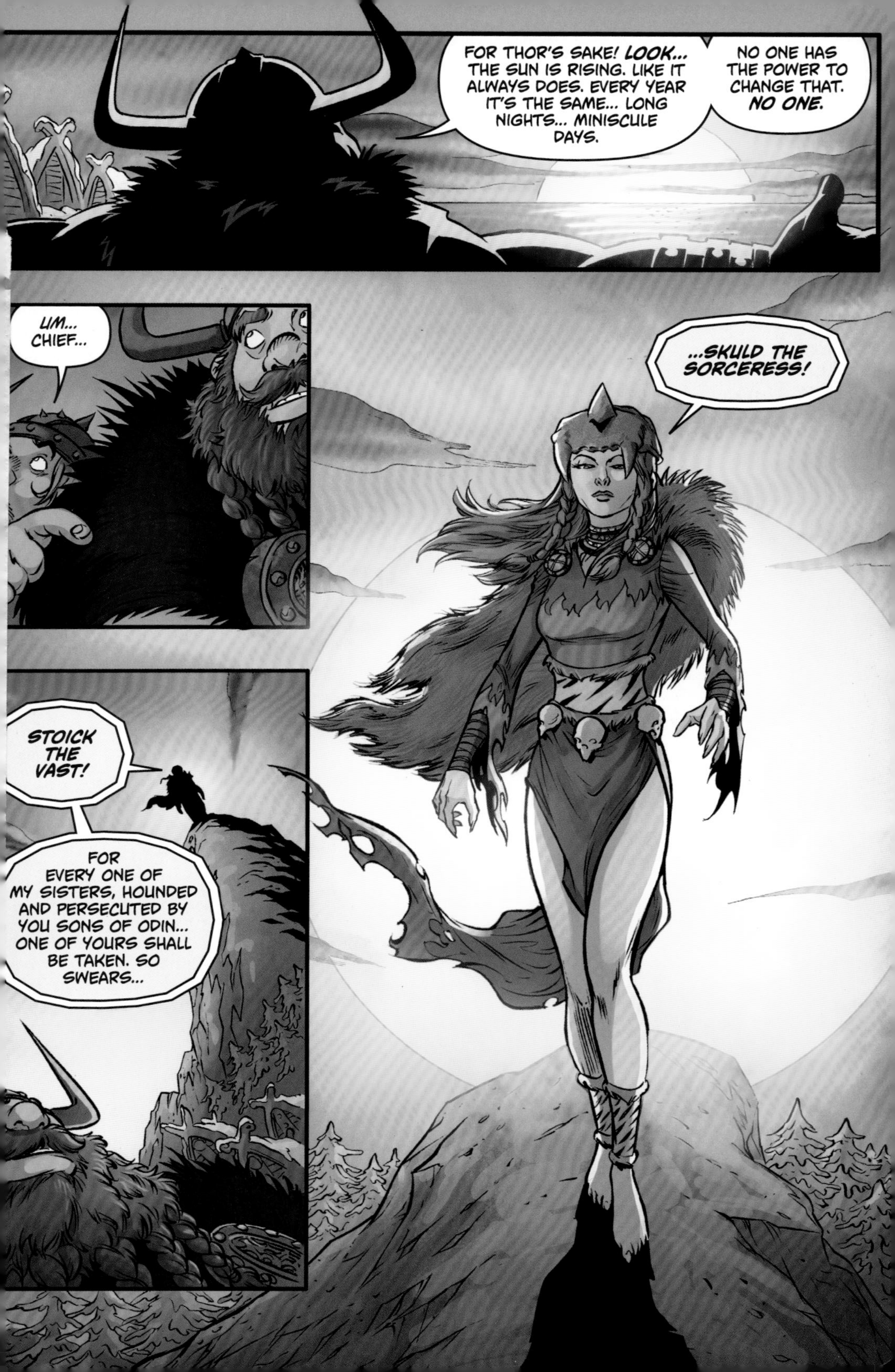
FOR THOR'S SAKE! LOOK... THE SUN IS RISING. LIKE IT ALWAYS DOES. EVERY YEAR IT'S THE SAME... LONG NIGHTS... MINISCULE DAYS.
NO ONE HAS THE POWER TO CHANGE THAT. NO ONE.
UM... CHIEF...
STOICK THE VAST!
FOR EVERY ONE OF MY SISTERS, HOUNDED AND PERSECUTED BY YOU SONS OF ODIN... ONE OF YOURS SHALL BE TAKEN. SO SWEARS...
...SKULD THE SORCERESS!

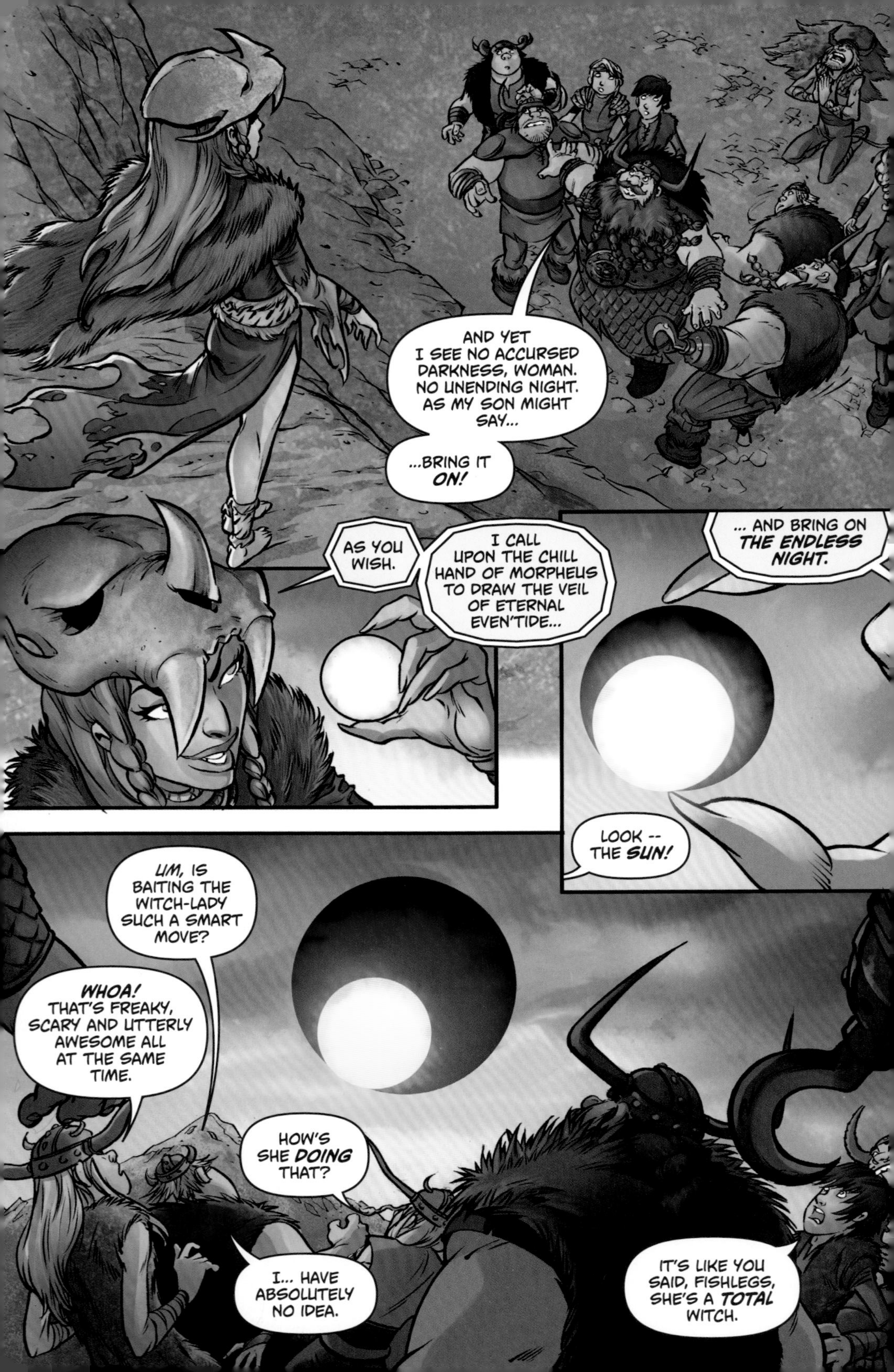
AND YET I SEE NO ACCURSED DARKNESS, WOMAN. NO UNENDING NIGHT. AS MY SON MIGHT SAY...
...BRING IT *ON!*
AS YOU WISH.
I CALL UPON THE CHILL HAND OF MORPHEUS TO DRAW THE VEIL OF ETERNAL EVEN'TIDE...
... AND BRING ON *THE ENDLESS NIGHT.*
LOOK -- THE *SUN!*
UM, IS BAITING THE WITCH-LADY SUCH A SMART MOVE?
WHOA! THAT'S FREAKY, SCARY AND UTTERLY AWESOME ALL AT THE SAME TIME.
HOW'S SHE *DOING* THAT?
I... HAVE ABSOLUTELY NO IDEA.
IT'S LIKE YOU SAID, FISHLEGS, SHE'S A *TOTAL* WITCH.

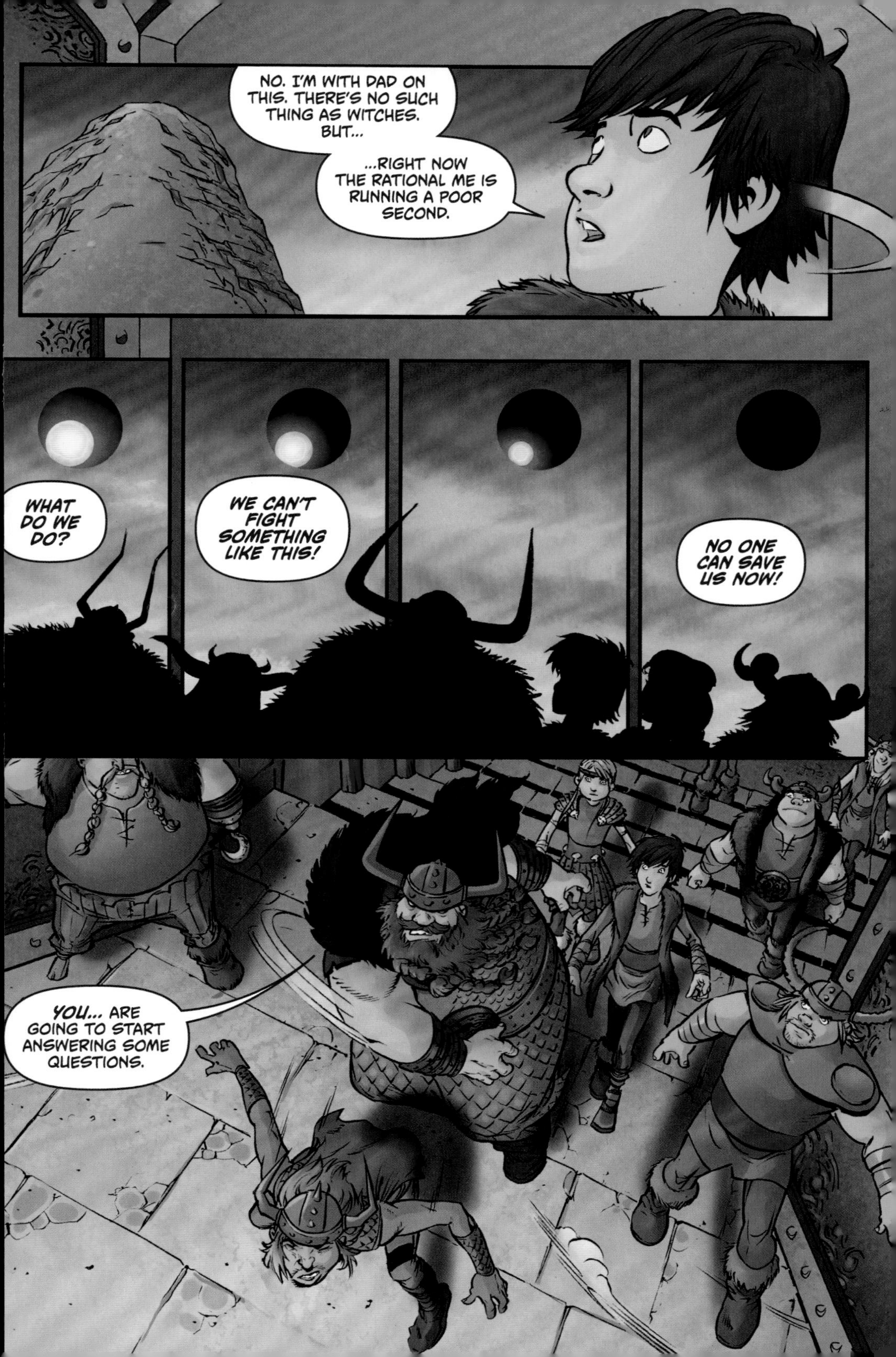
NO. I'M WITH DAD ON THIS. THERE'S NO SUCH THING AS WITCHES. BUT...
...RIGHT NOW THE RATIONAL ME IS RUNNING A POOR SECOND.
WHAT DO WE DO?
WE CAN'T FIGHT SOMETHING LIKE THIS!
NO ONE CAN SAVE US NOW!
YOU... ARE GOING TO START ANSWERING SOME QUESTIONS.

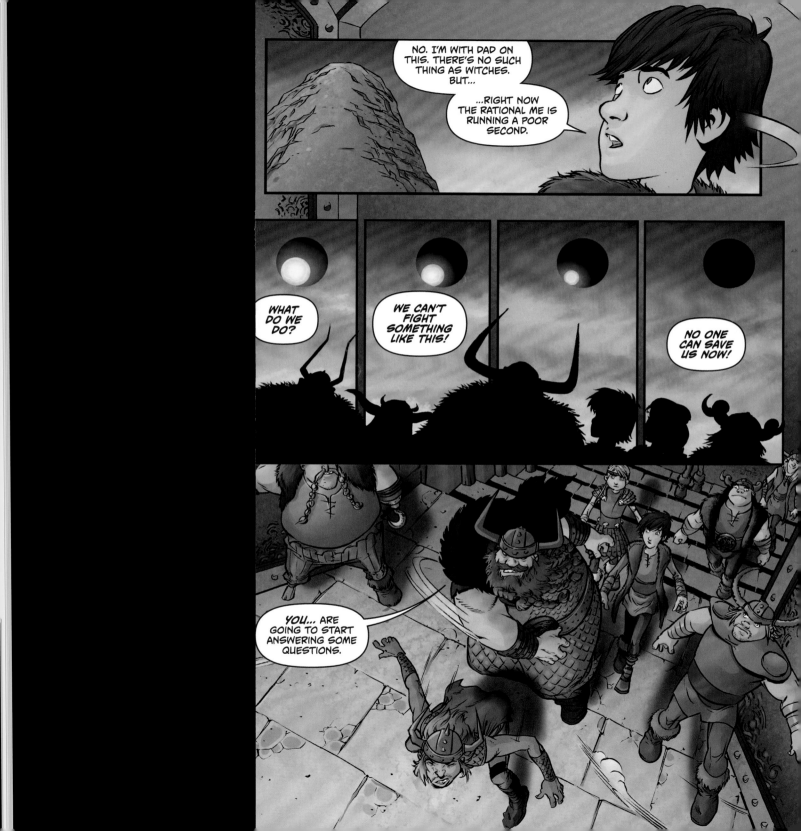

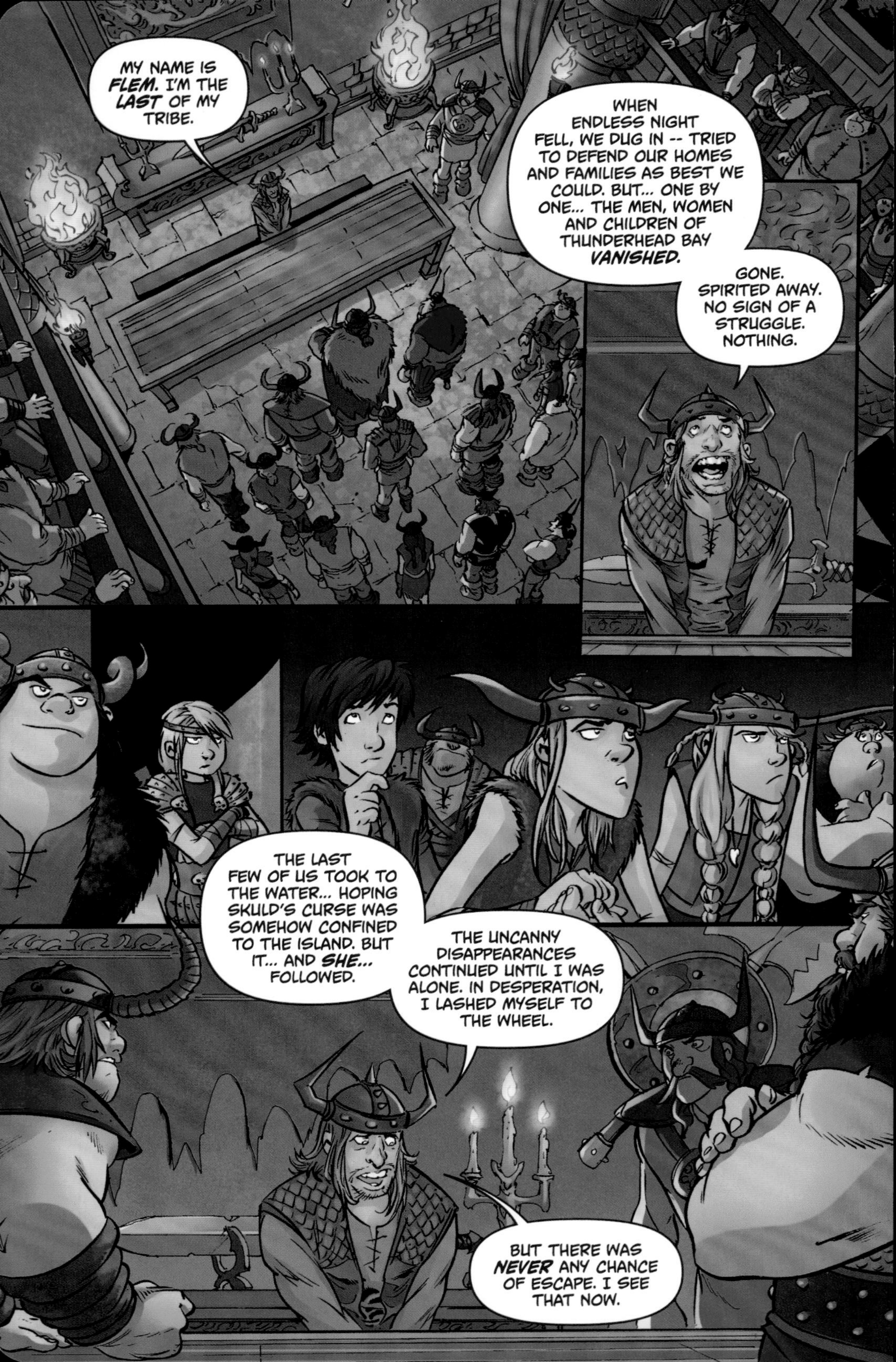
MY NAME IS FLEM. I'M THE LAST OF MY TRIBE.
WHEN ENDLESS NIGHT FELL, WE DUG IN -- TRIED TO DEFEND OUR HOMES AND FAMILIES AS BEST WE COULD. BUT... ONE BY ONE... THE MEN, WOMEN AND CHILDREN OF THUNDERHEAD BAY VANISHED.
GONE. SPIRITED AWAY. NO SIGN OF A STRUGGLE. NOTHING.
THE LAST FEW OF US TOOK TO THE WATER... HOPING SKULD'S CURSE WAS SOMEHOW CONFINED TO THE ISLAND. BUT IT... AND SHE... FOLLOWED.
THE UNCANNY DISAPPEARANCES CONTINUED UNTIL I WAS ALONE. IN DESPERATION, I LASHED MYSELF TO THE WHEEL.
BUT THERE WAS NEVER ANY CHANCE OF ESCAPE. I SEE THAT NOW.

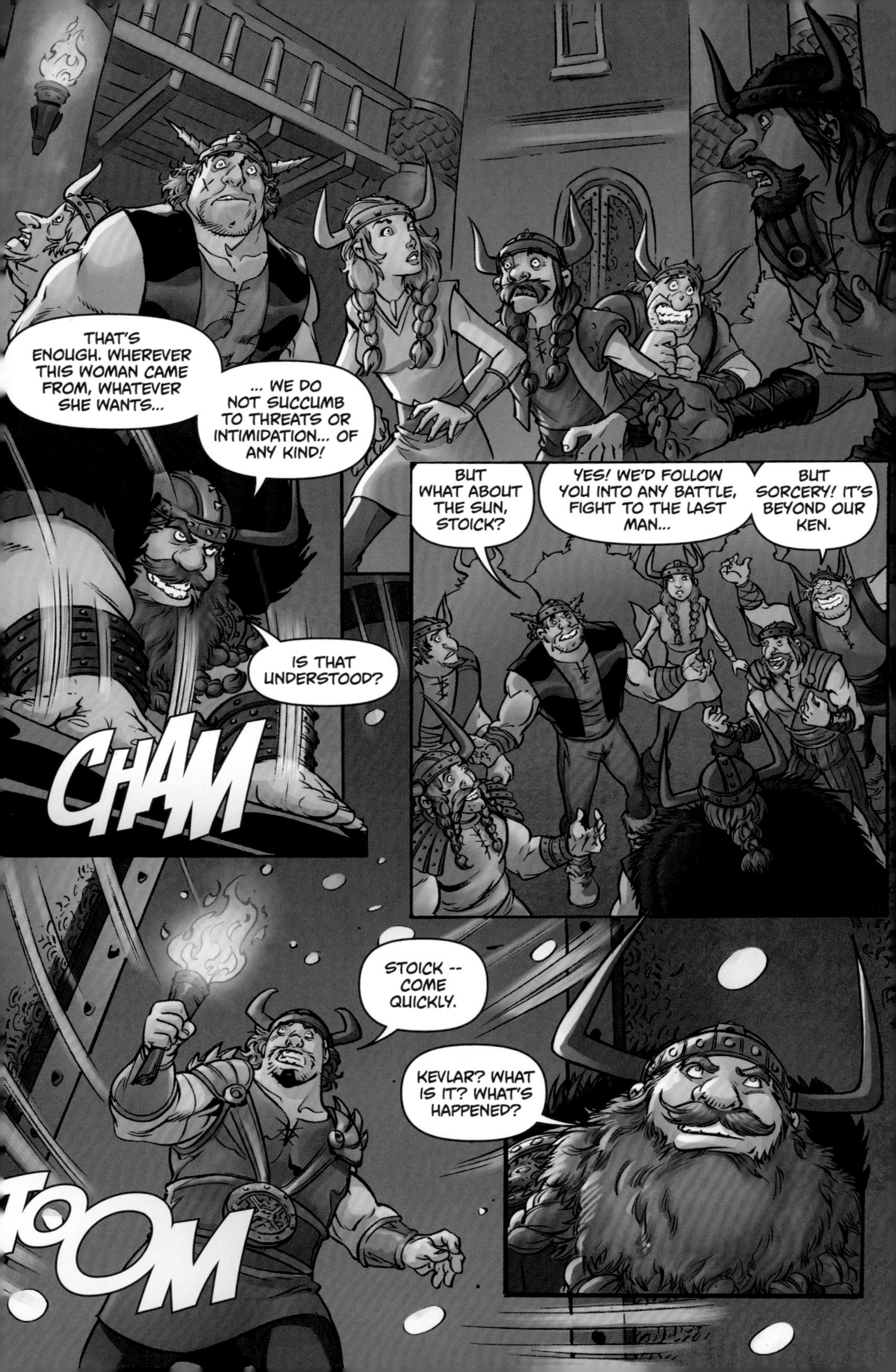
THAT'S ENOUGH. WHEREVER THIS WOMAN CAME FROM, WHATEVER SHE WANTS...
... WE DO NOT SUCCUMB TO THREATS OR INTIMIDATION... OF ANY KIND!
IS THAT UNDERSTOOD?
CHAM
BUT WHAT ABOUT THE SUN, STOICK?
YES! WE'D FOLLOW YOU INTO ANY BATTLE, FIGHT TO THE LAST MAN...
BUT SORCERY! IT'S BEYOND OUR KEN.
STOICK -- COME QUICKLY.
KEVLAR? WHAT IS IT? WHAT'S HAPPENED?
TOOM

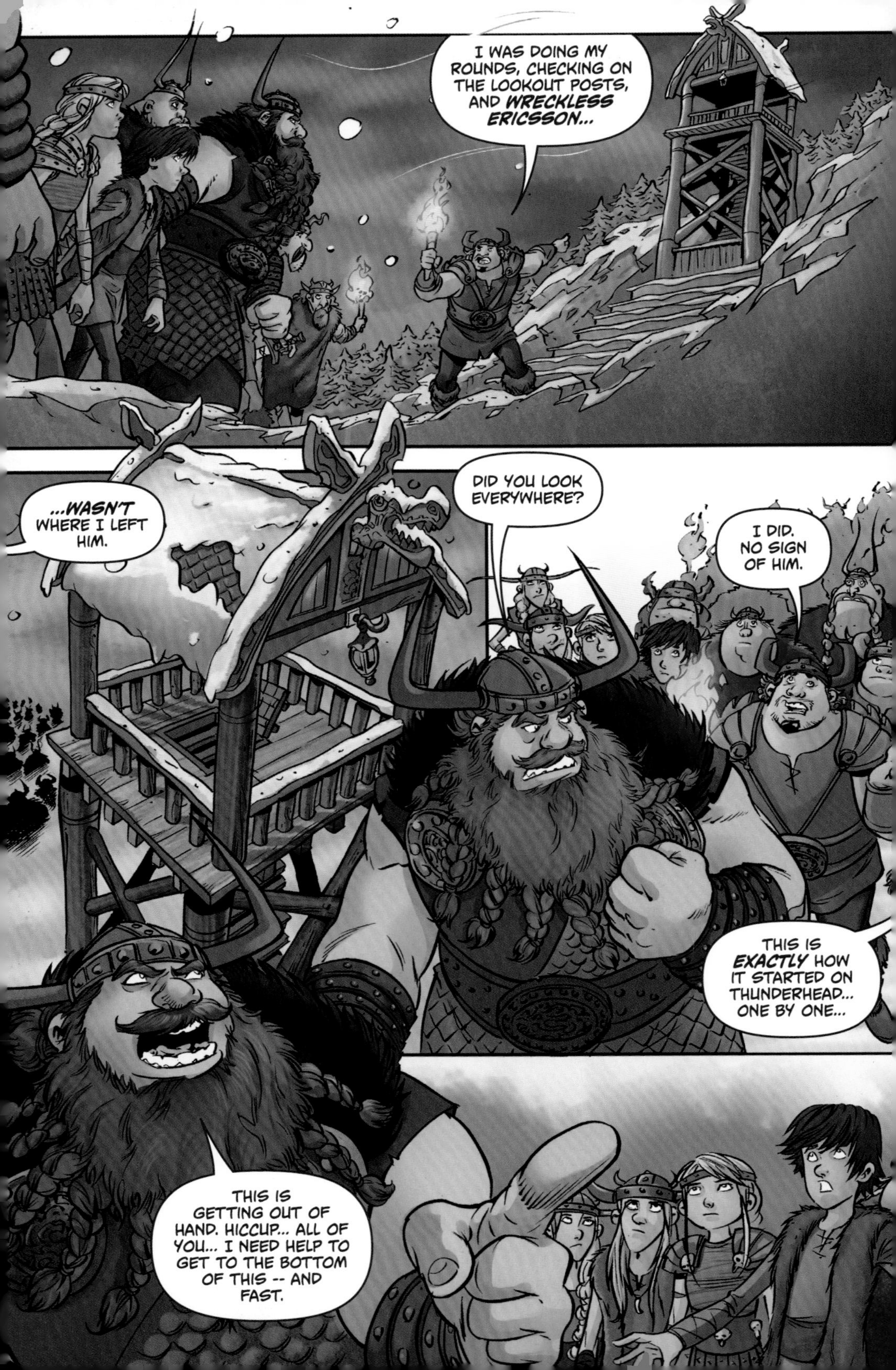
I WAS DOING MY ROUNDS, CHECKING ON THE LOOKOUT POSTS, AND WRECKLESS ERICSSON...
...WASN'T WHERE I LEFT HIM.
DID YOU LOOK EVERYWHERE?
I DID. NO SIGN OF HIM.
THIS IS EXACTLY HOW IT STARTED ON THUNDERHEAD... ONE BY ONE...
THIS IS GETTING OUT OF HAND. HICCUP... ALL OF YOU... I NEED HELP TO GET TO THE BOTTOM OF THIS -- AND FAST.

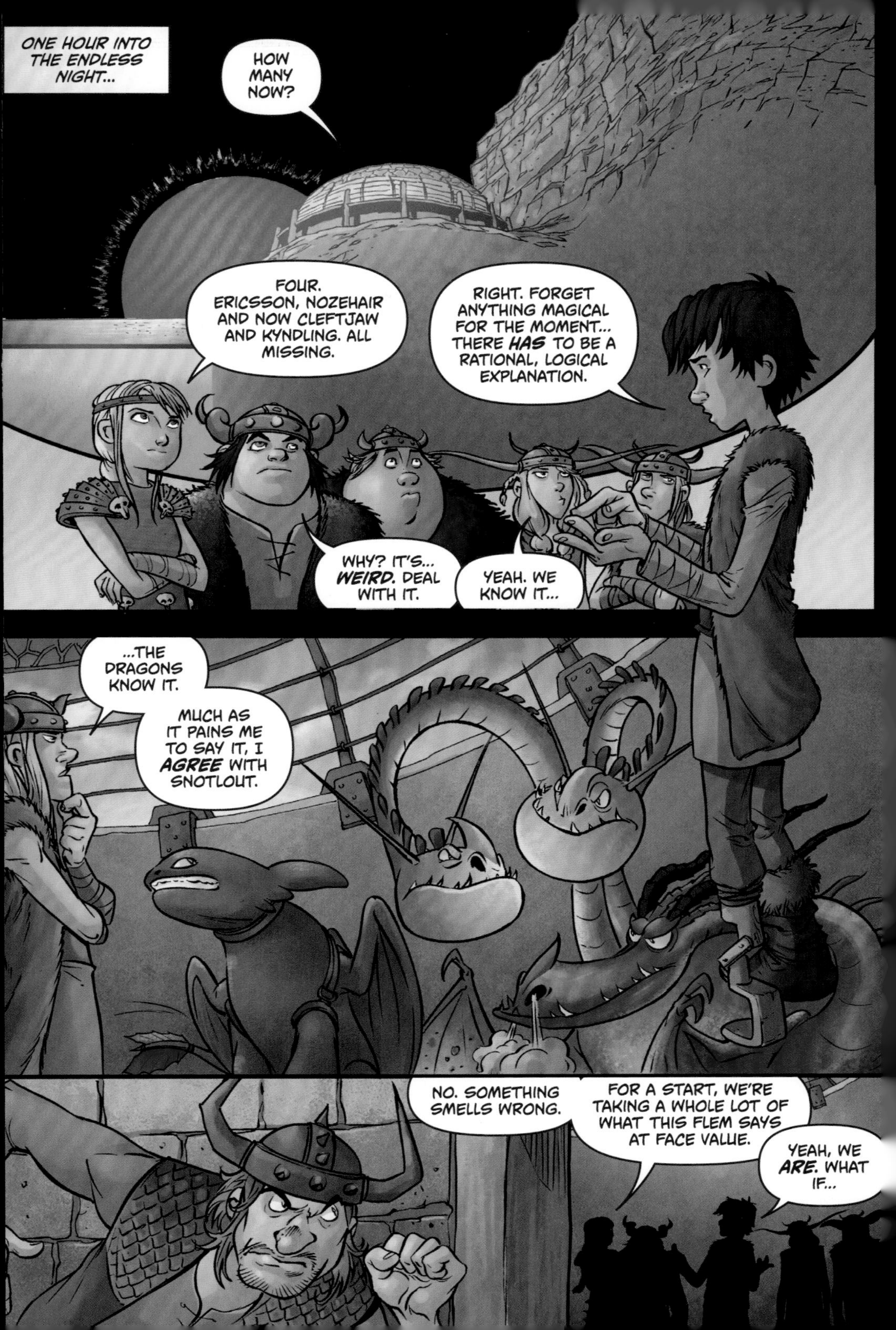
ONE HOUR INTO THE ENDLESS NIGHT...
HOW MANY NOW?
FOUR. ERICSSON, NOZEHAIR AND NOW CLEFTJAW AND KYNDLING. ALL MISSING.
RIGHT. FORGET ANYTHING MAGICAL FOR THE MOMENT... THERE **HAS** TO BE A RATIONAL, LOGICAL EXPLANATION.
WHY? IT'S... **WEIRD.** DEAL WITH IT.
YEAH. WE KNOW IT...
...THE DRAGONS KNOW IT.
MUCH AS IT PAINS ME TO SAY IT, I **AGREE** WITH SNOTLOUT.
NO. SOMETHING SMELLS WRONG.
FOR A START, WE'RE TAKING A WHOLE LOT OF WHAT THIS FLEM SAYS AT FACE VALUE.
YEAH, WE **ARE**. WHAT IF...

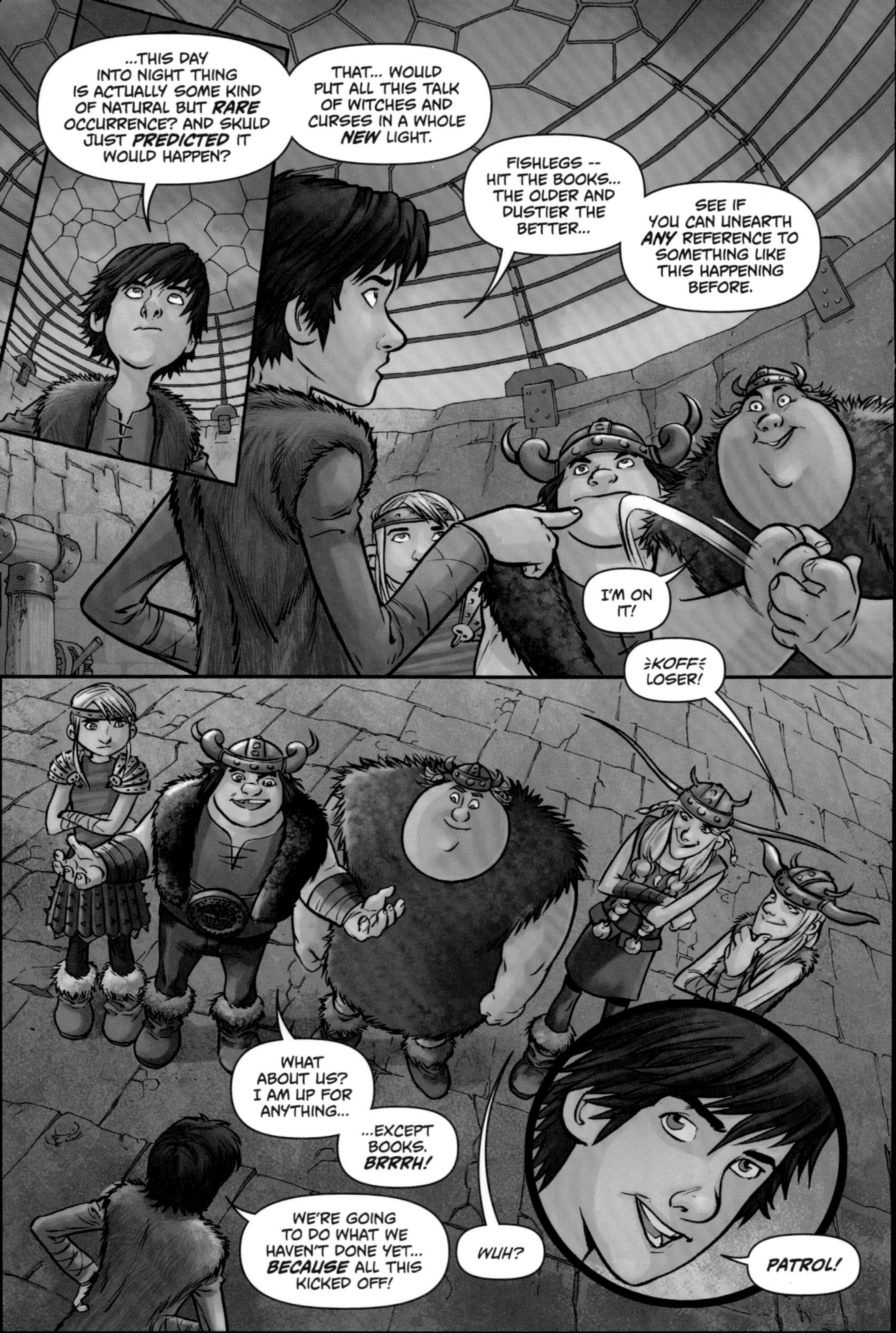
...THIS DAY INTO NIGHT THING IS ACTUALLY SOME KIND OF NATURAL BUT *RARE* OCCURRENCE? AND SKULD JUST *PREDICTED* IT WOULD HAPPEN?
THAT... WOULD PUT ALL THIS TALK OF WITCHES AND CURSES IN A WHOLE *NEW* LIGHT.
FISHLEGS -- HIT THE BOOKS... THE OLDER AND DUSTIER THE BETTER...
SEE IF YOU CAN UNEARTH *ANY* REFERENCE TO SOMETHING LIKE THIS HAPPENING BEFORE.
I'M ON IT!
KOFF LOSER!
WHAT ABOUT US? I AM UP FOR ANYTHING...
...EXCEPT BOOKS. *BRRRH!*
WE'RE GOING TO DO WHAT WE HAVEN'T DONE YET... *BECAUSE* ALL THIS KICKED OFF!
WUH?
PATROL!

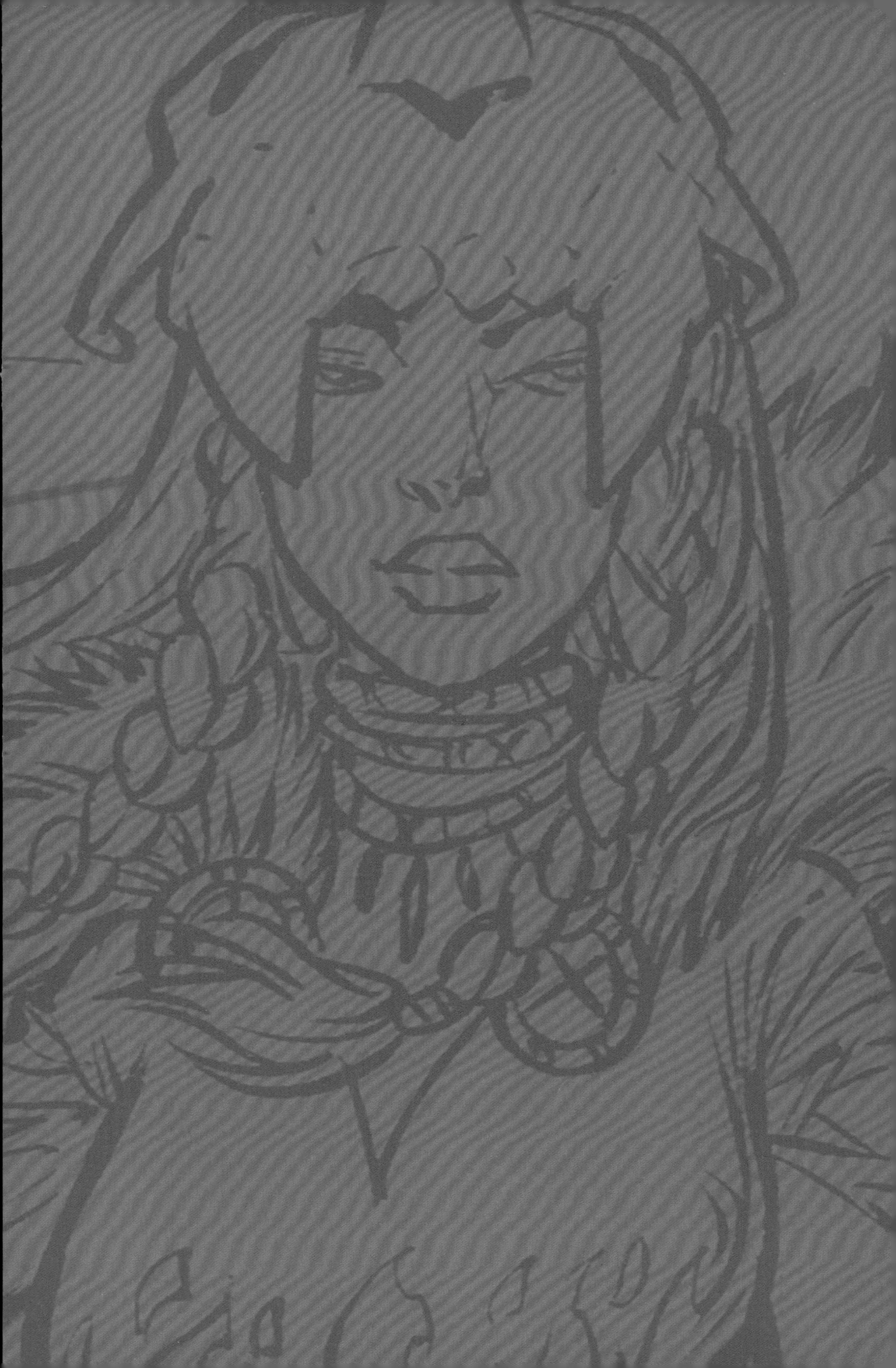

CHAPTER THREE

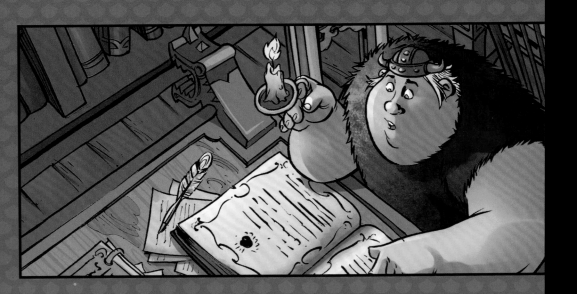

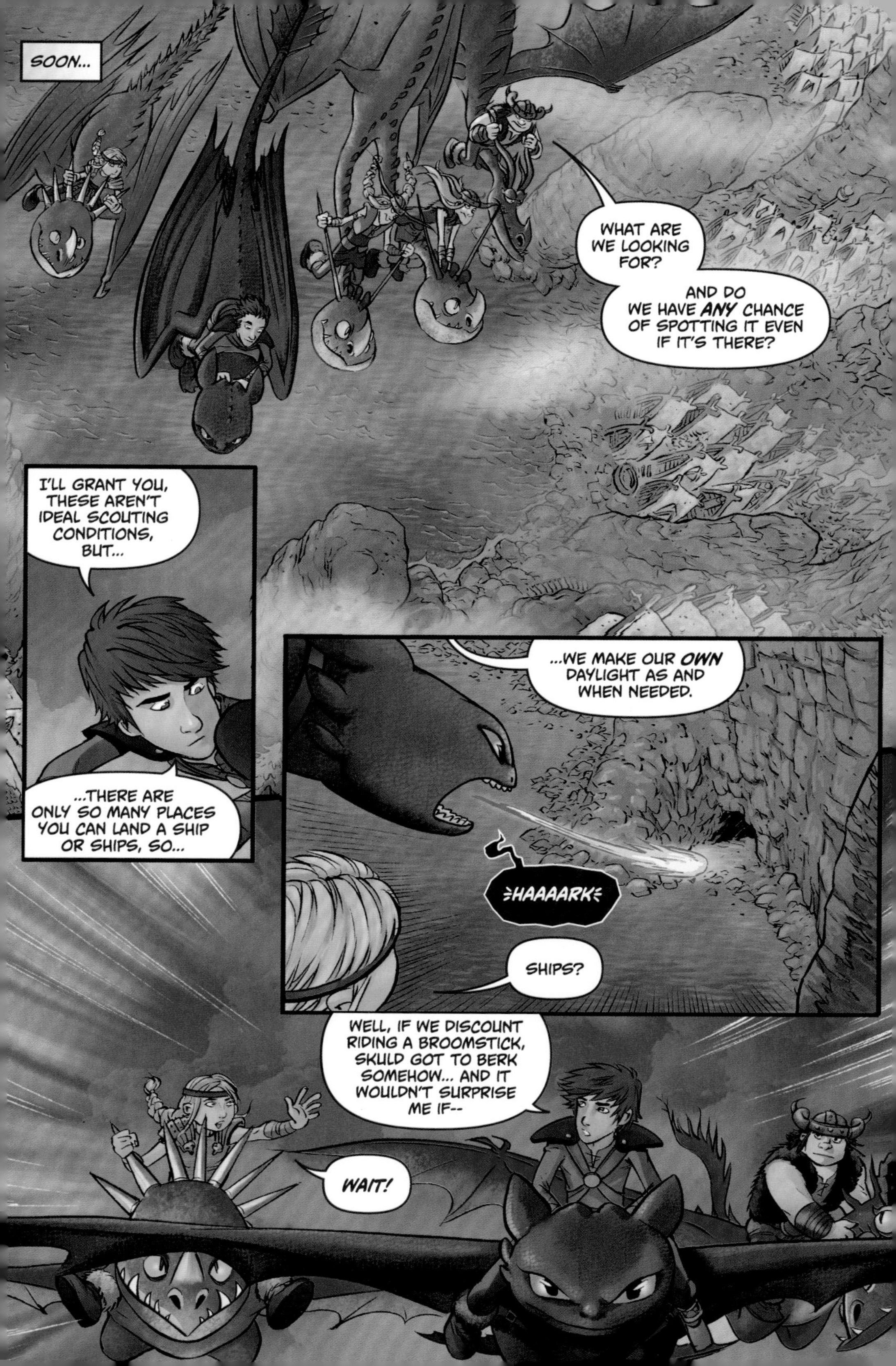
SOON...
WHAT ARE WE LOOKING FOR?
AND DO WE HAVE ANY CHANCE OF SPOTTING IT EVEN IF IT'S THERE?
I'LL GRANT YOU, THESE AREN'T IDEAL SCOUTING CONDITIONS, BUT...
...THERE ARE ONLY SO MANY PLACES YOU CAN LAND A SHIP OR SHIPS, SO...
...WE MAKE OUR OWN DAYLIGHT AS AND WHEN NEEDED.
HAAAARK
SHIPS?
WELL, IF WE DISCOUNT RIDING A BROOMSTICK, SKULD GOT TO BERK SOMEHOW... AND IT WOULDN'T SURPRISE ME IF--
WAIT!

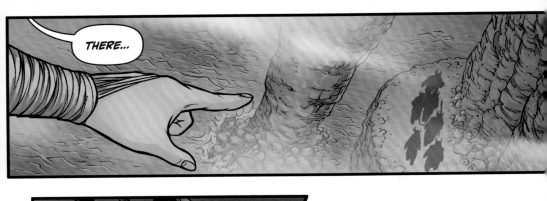

THERE...

HANG BACK... I'M GOING IN FOR A CLOSER LOOK.

TOOTHLESS -- STEALTH MODE.

CLEFTJAW AND NOZEHAIR. PLUS ARMED ESCORT.

NOT VANISHED -- TAKEN PRISONER.

WHAT NOW?

THEY'RE HEADED FOR *PITFALL COVE*. AND WE...

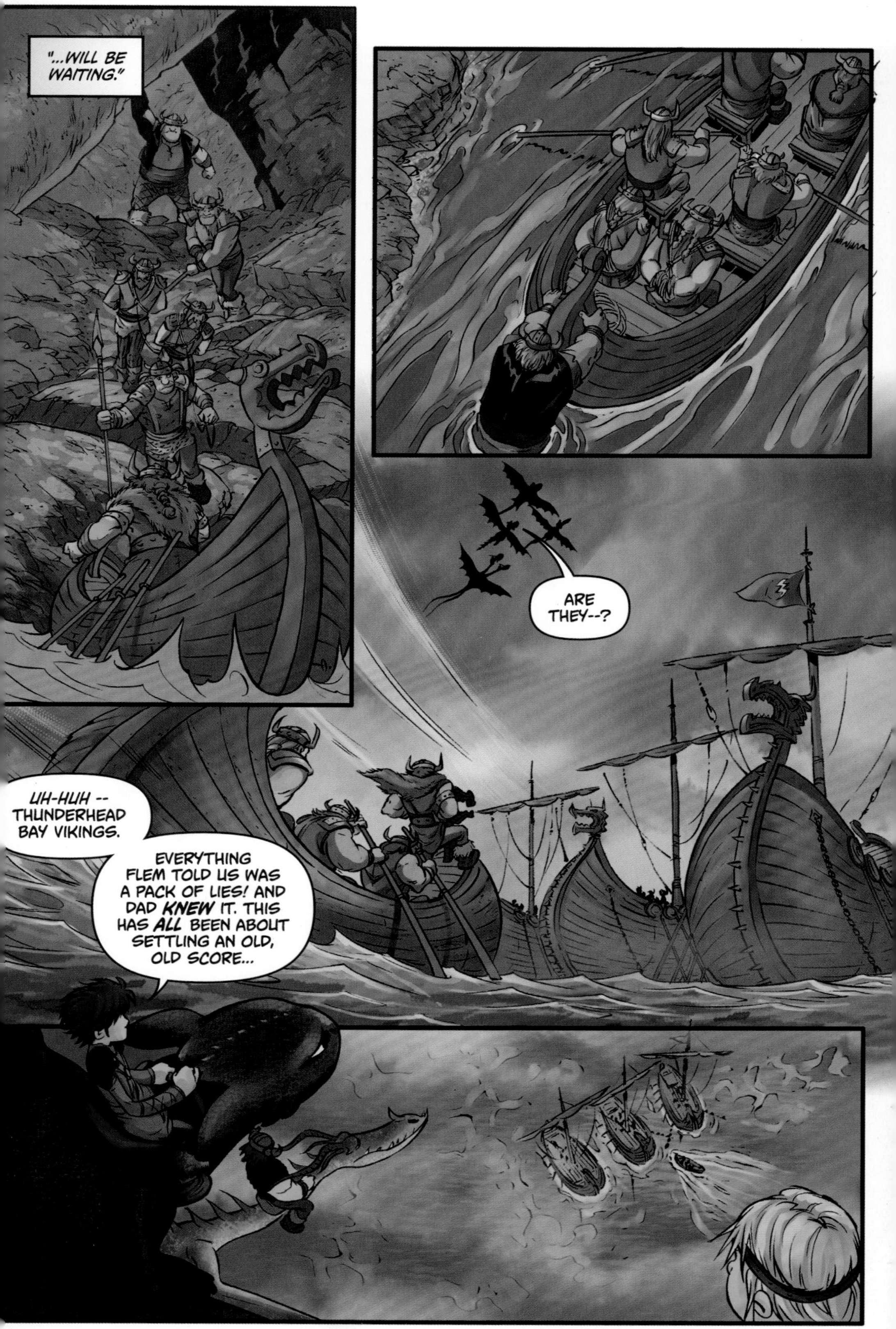
"...WILL BE WAITING."
ARE THEY--?
UH-HUH -- THUNDERHEAD BAY VIKINGS.
EVERYTHING FLEM TOLD US WAS A PACK OF LIES! AND DAD KNEW IT. THIS HAS ALL BEEN ABOUT SETTLING AN OLD, OLD SCORE...

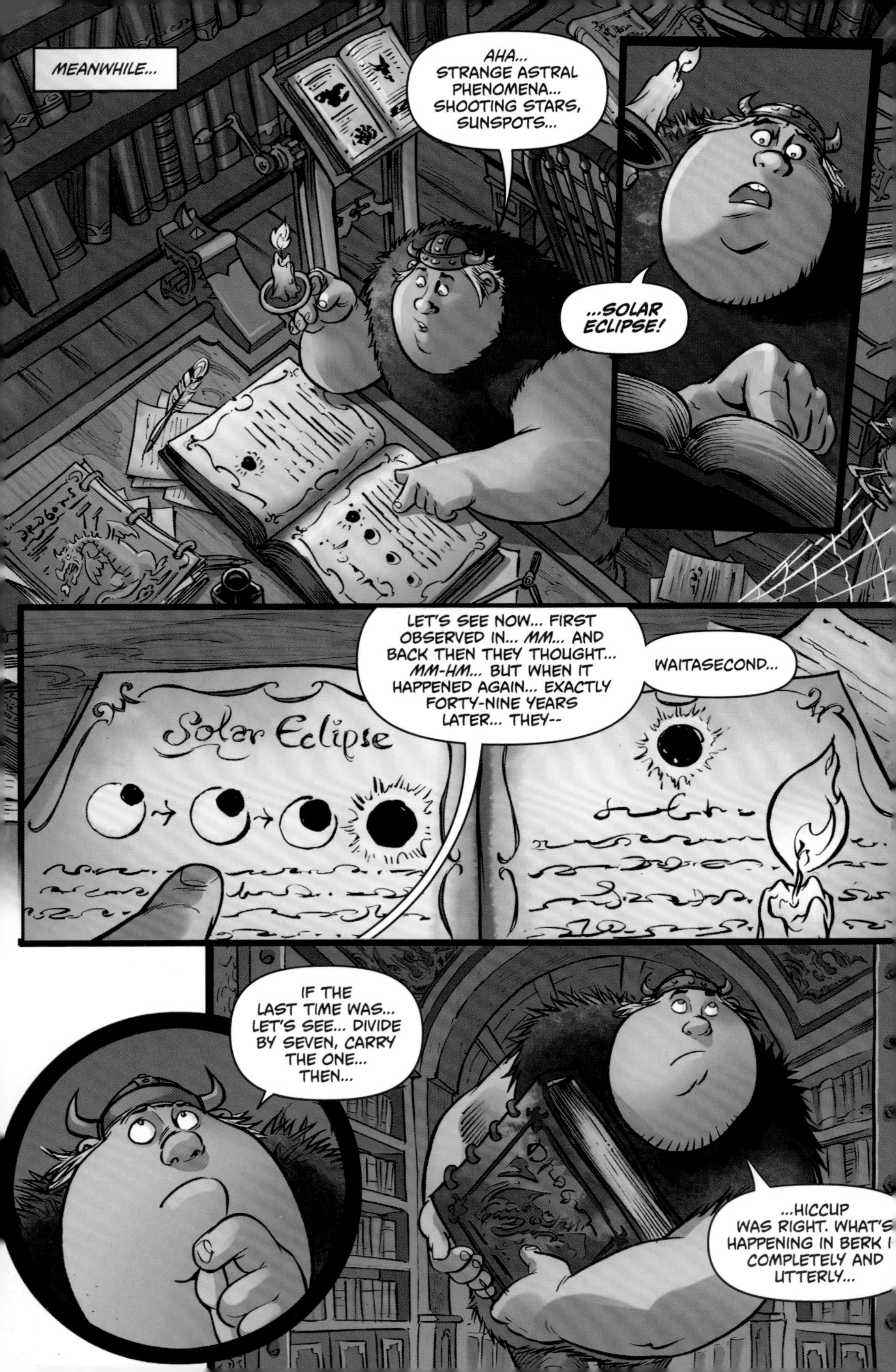
MEANWHILE...
AHA... STRANGE ASTRAL PHENOMENA... SHOOTING STARS, SUNSPOTS...
...SOLAR ECLIPSE!
LET'S SEE NOW... FIRST OBSERVED IN... MM... AND BACK THEN THEY THOUGHT... MM-HM... BUT WHEN IT HAPPENED AGAIN... EXACTLY FORTY-NINE YEARS LATER... THEY--
WAITASECOND...
Solar Eclipse
IF THE LAST TIME WAS... LET'S SEE... DIVIDE BY SEVEN, CARRY THE ONE... THEN...
...HICCUP WAS RIGHT. WHAT'S HAPPENING IN BERK I COMPLETELY AND UTTERLY...

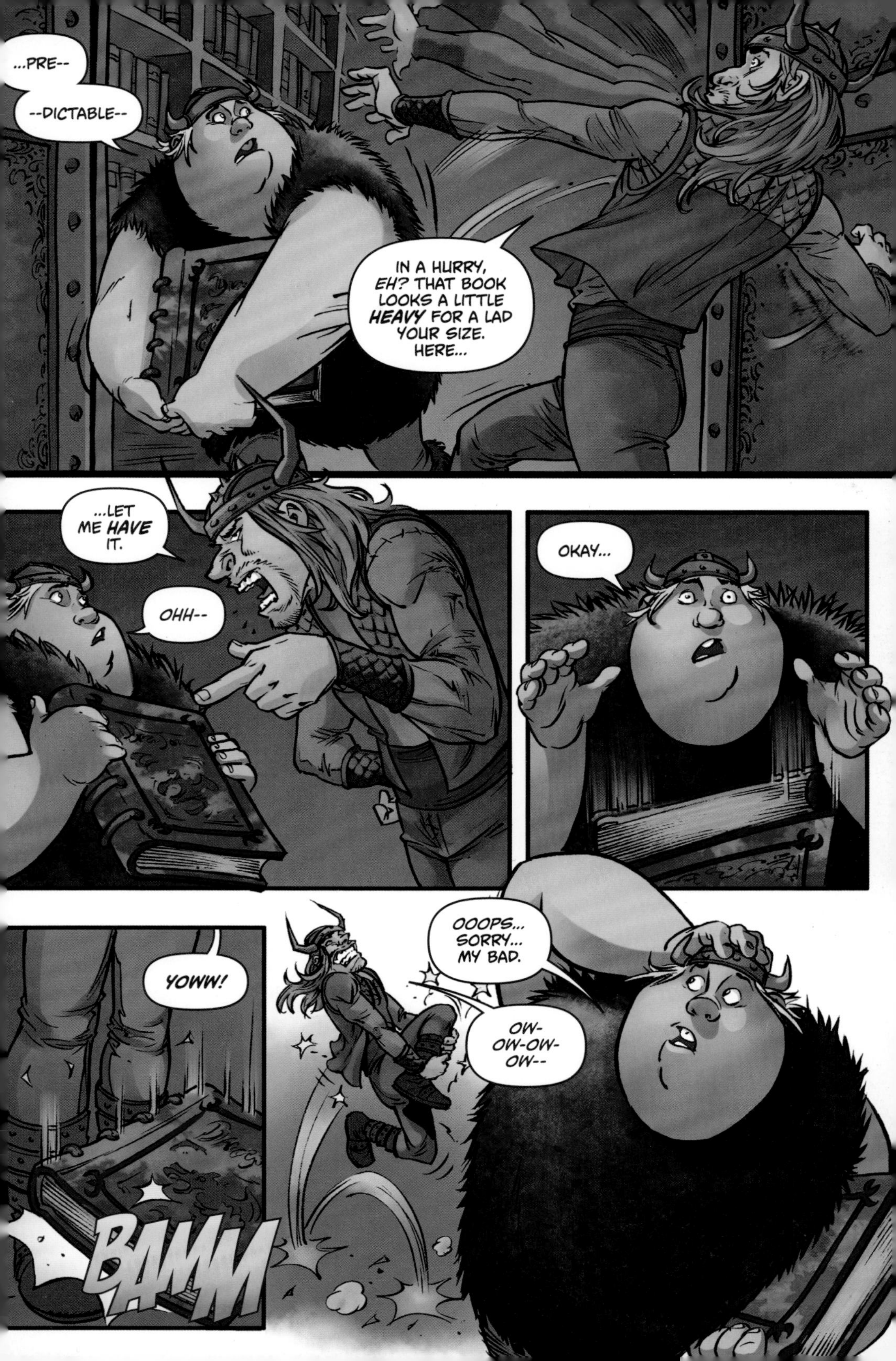
...PRE--
--DICTABLE--
IN A HURRY, EH? THAT BOOK LOOKS A LITTLE HEAVY FOR A LAD YOUR SIZE. HERE...
...LET ME HAVE IT.
OHH--
OKAY...
YOWW!
OOOPS... SORRY... MY BAD.
OW-OW-OW-OW--
BAMM

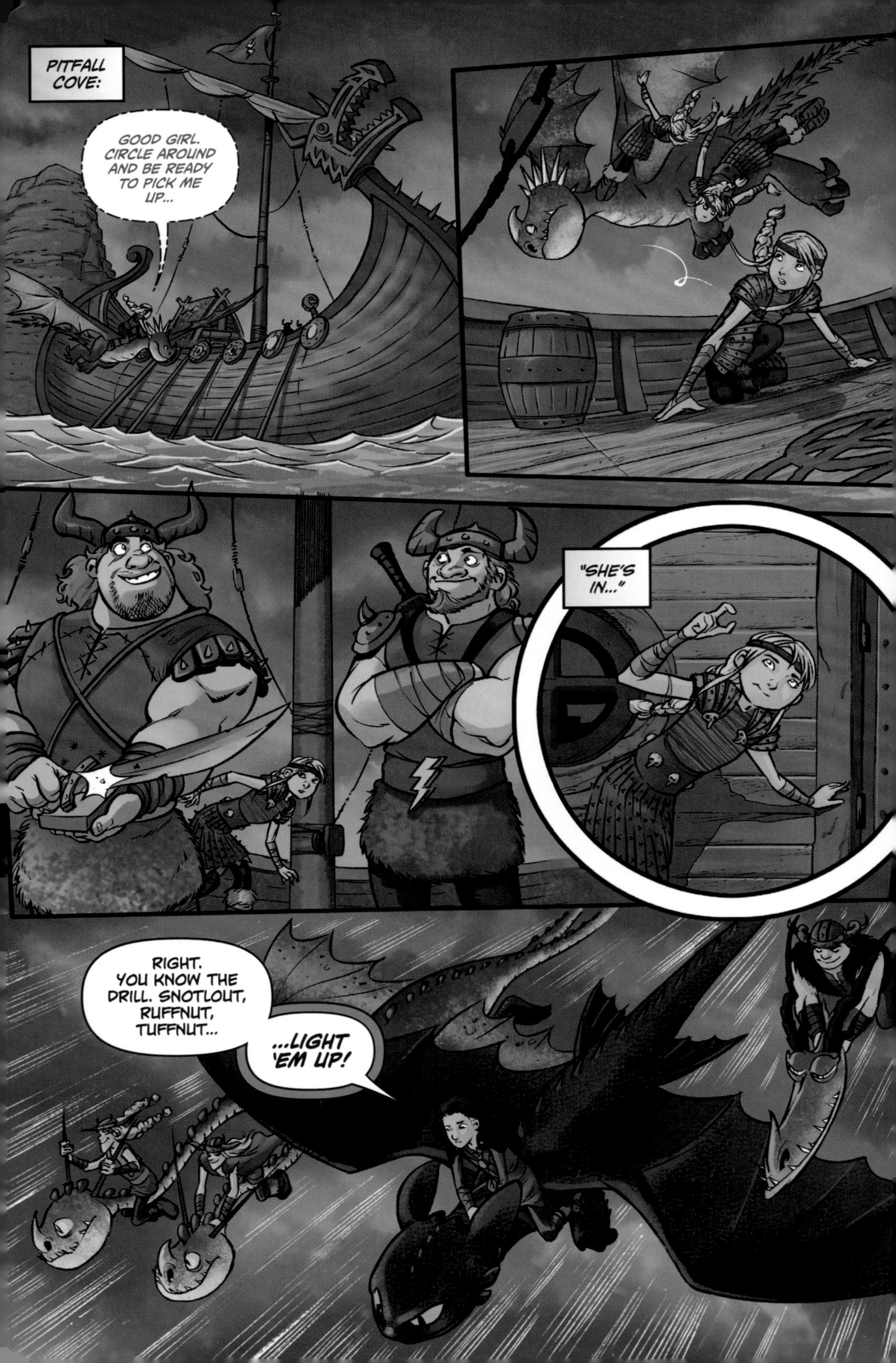
PITFALL COVE:
GOOD GIRL. CIRCLE AROUND AND BE READY TO PICK ME UP...
"SHE'S IN..."
RIGHT. YOU KNOW THE DRILL. SNOTLOUT, RUFFNUT, TUFFNUT...
...LIGHT 'EM UP!

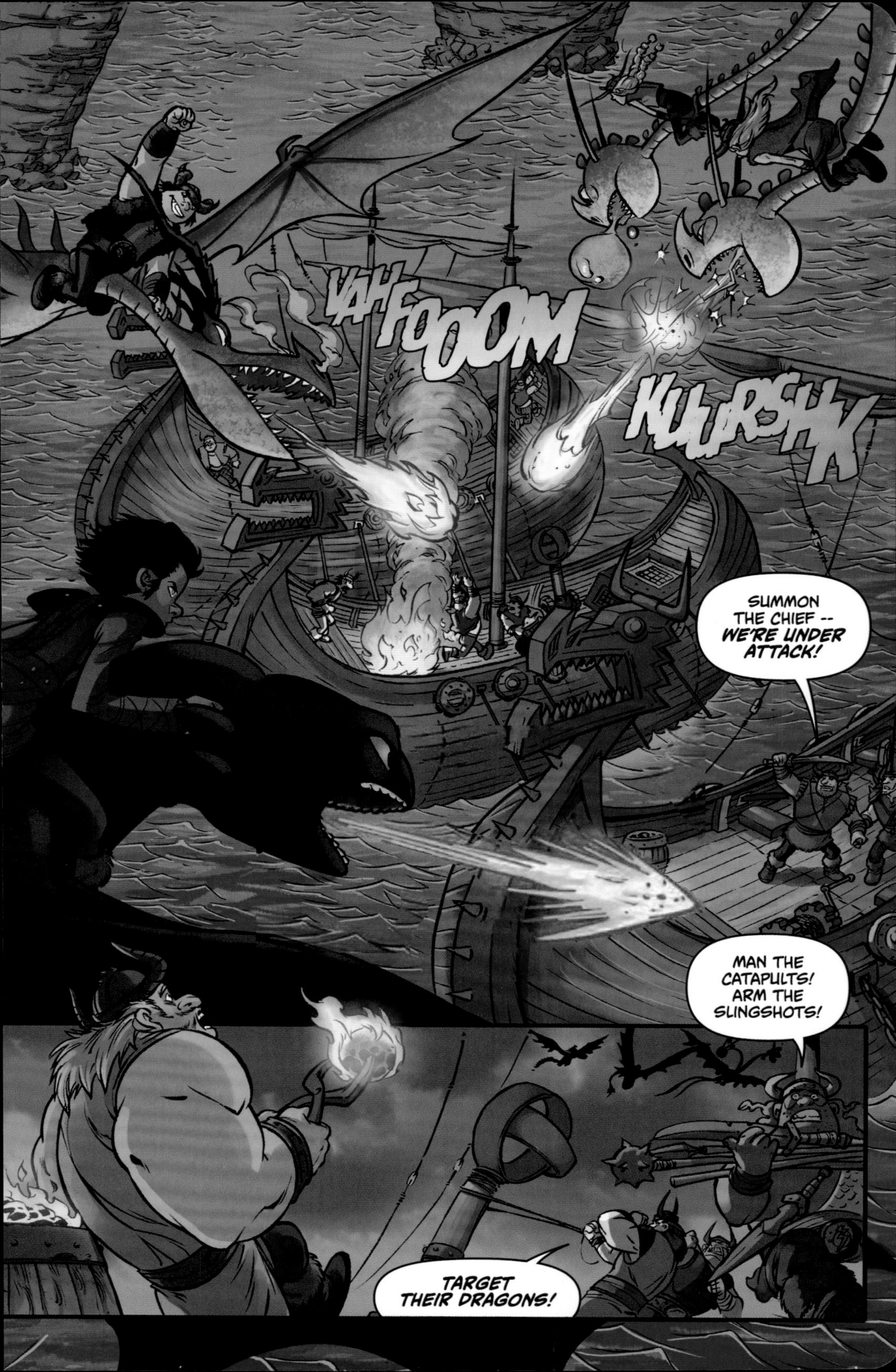

VAHFOOOM
KUURSHK
SUMMON THE CHIEF -- WE'RE UNDER ATTACK!
MAN THE CATAPULTS! ARM THE SLINGSHOTS!
TARGET THEIR DRAGONS!

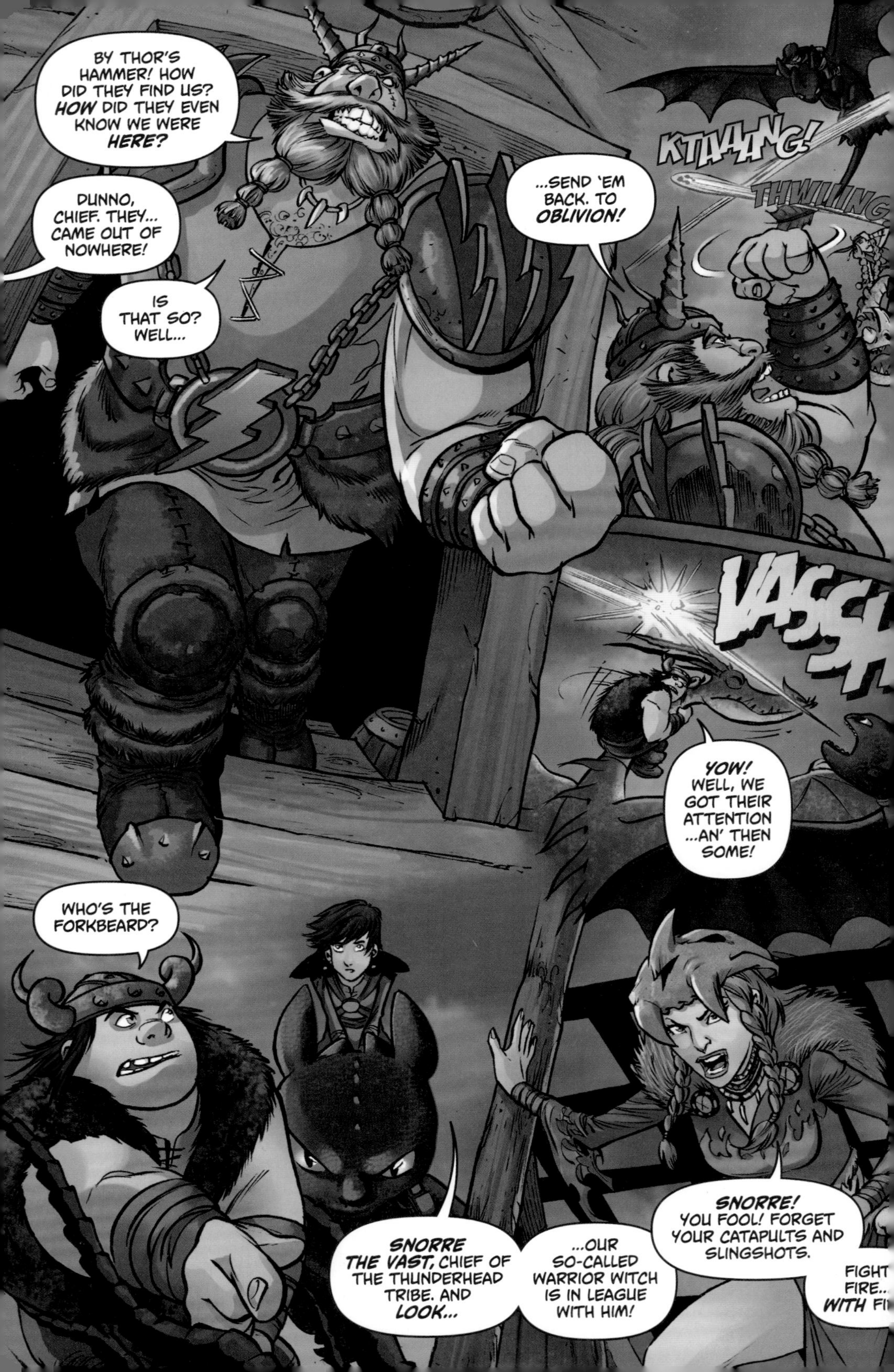
BY THOR'S HAMMER! HOW DID THEY FIND US? HOW DID THEY EVEN KNOW WE WERE HERE?
DUNNO, CHIEF. THEY... CAME OUT OF NOWHERE!
IS THAT SO? WELL...
...SEND 'EM BACK. TO OBLIVION!
KTVAAANG!
THWIIING
VASSH
YOW! WELL, WE GOT THEIR ATTENTION ...AN' THEN SOME!
WHO'S THE FORKBEARD?
SNORRE THE VAST, CHIEF OF THE THUNDERHEAD TRIBE. AND LOOK...
...OUR SO-CALLED WARRIOR WITCH IS IN LEAGUE WITH HIM!
SNORRE! YOU FOOL! FORGET YOUR CATAPULTS AND SLINGSHOTS.
FIGHT FIRE... WITH FI

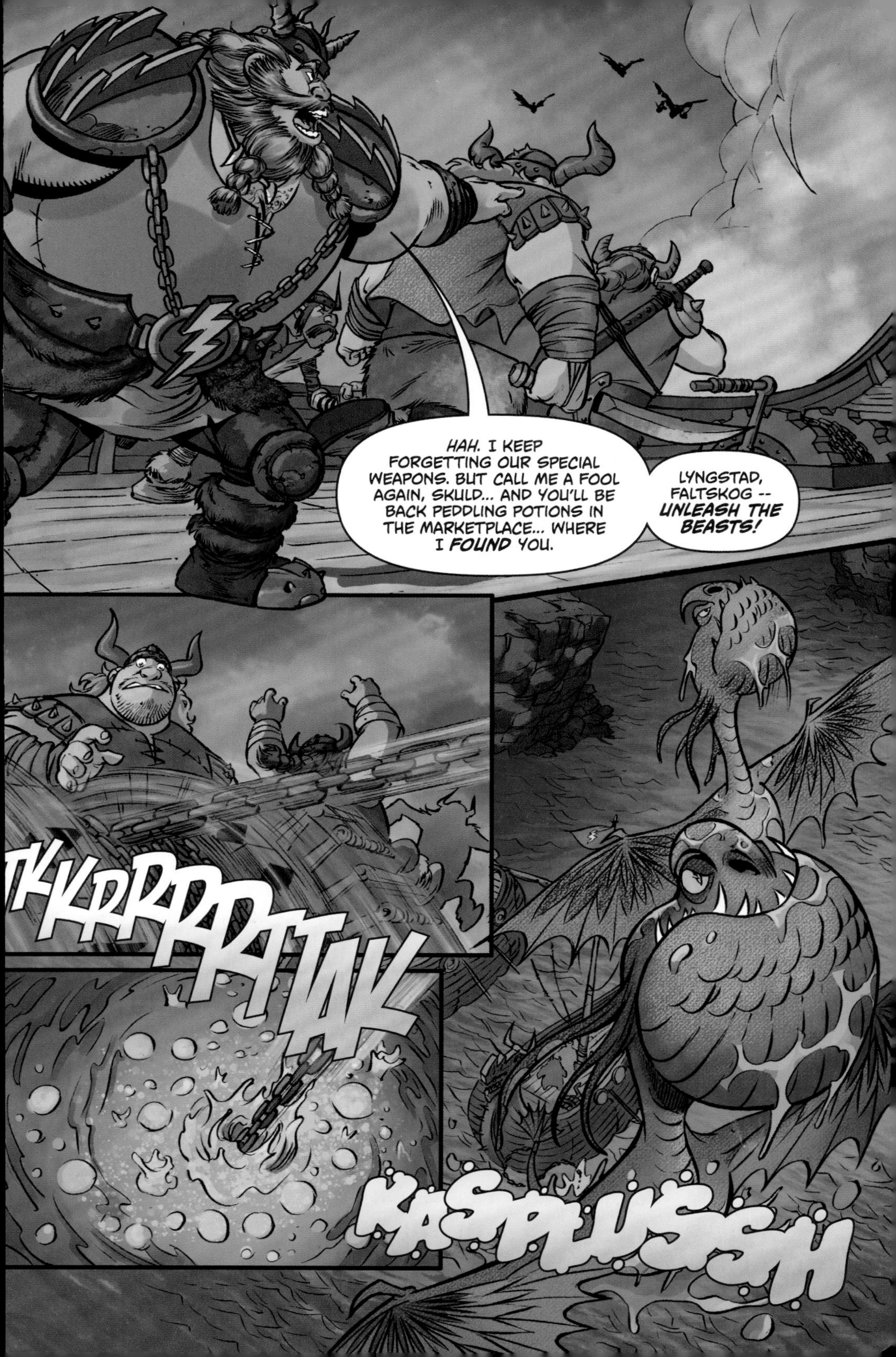
HAH. I KEEP FORGETTING OUR SPECIAL WEAPONS. BUT CALL ME A FOOL AGAIN, SKULD... AND YOU'LL BE BACK PEDDLING POTIONS IN THE MARKETPLACE... WHERE I *FOUND* YOU.
LYNGSTAD, FALTSKOG -- ***UNLEASH THE BEASTS!***
TKKRRRRRTTAK
KASPLUSSSH

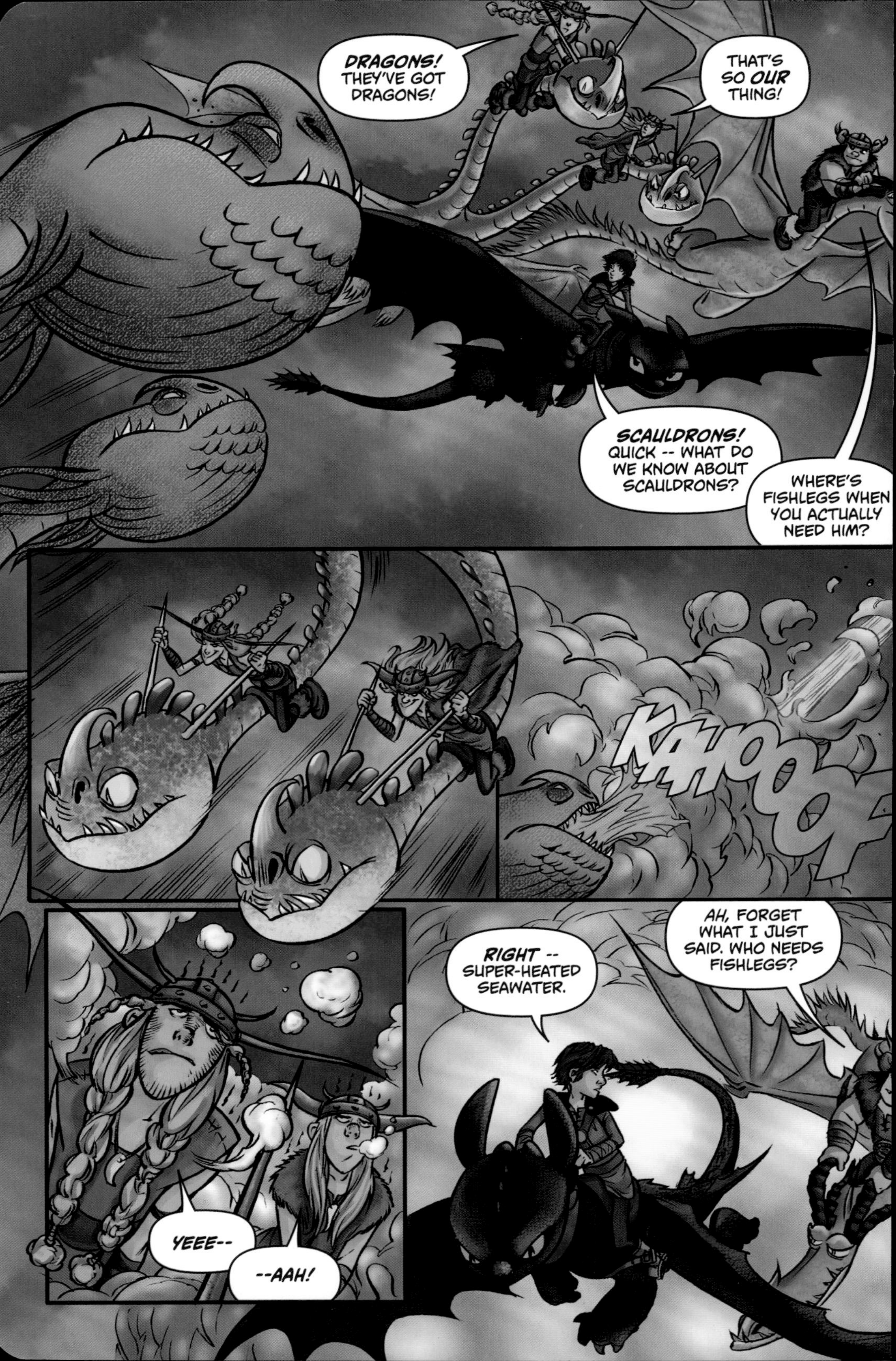
DRAGONS! THEY'VE GOT DRAGONS!
THAT'S SO OUR THING!
SCAULDRONS! QUICK -- WHAT DO WE KNOW ABOUT SCAULDRONS?
WHERE'S FISHLEGS WHEN YOU ACTUALLY NEED HIM?
KAHOOOF
YEEE--
--AAH!
RIGHT -- SUPER-HEATED SEAWATER.
AH, FORGET WHAT I JUST SAID. WHO NEEDS FISHLEGS?

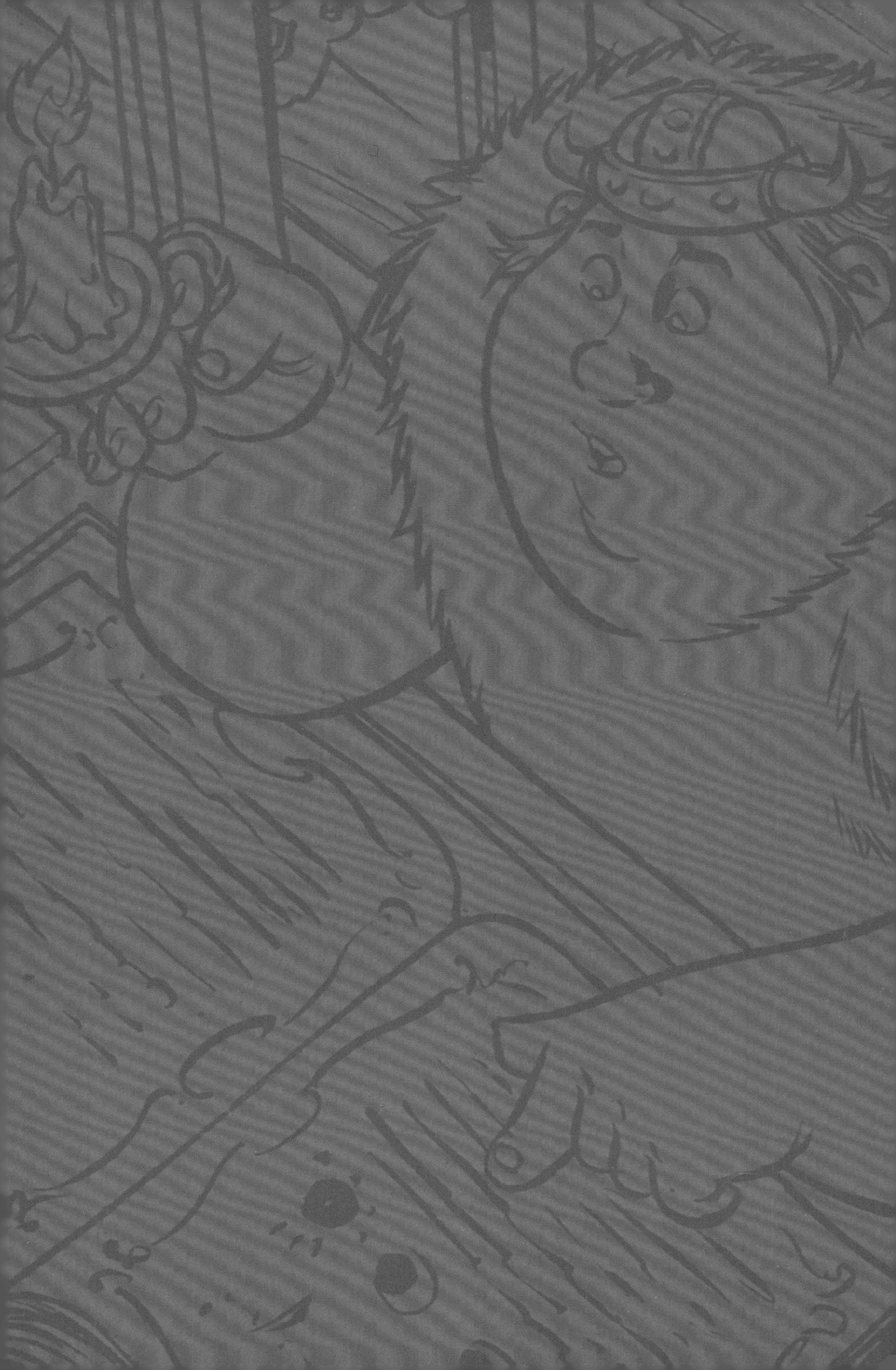

CHAPTER FOUR

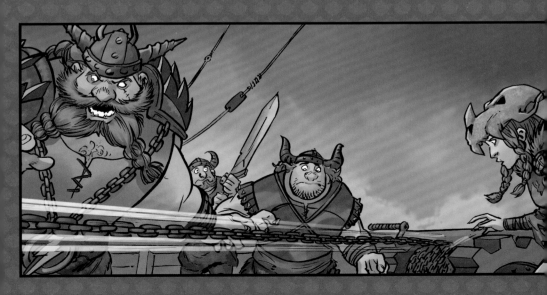

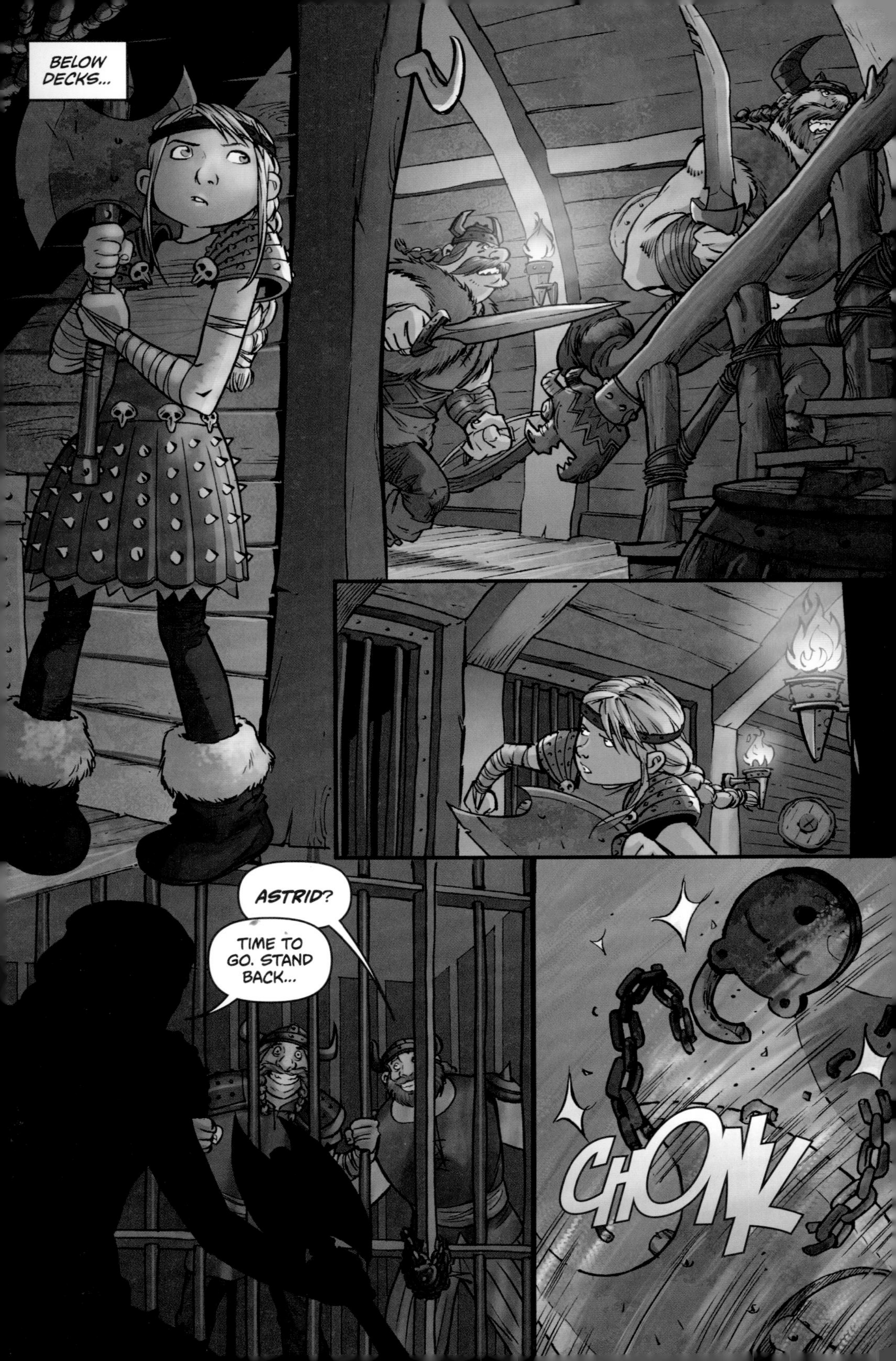
BELOW DECKS...
ASTRID?
TIME TO GO. STAND BACK...
CHONK

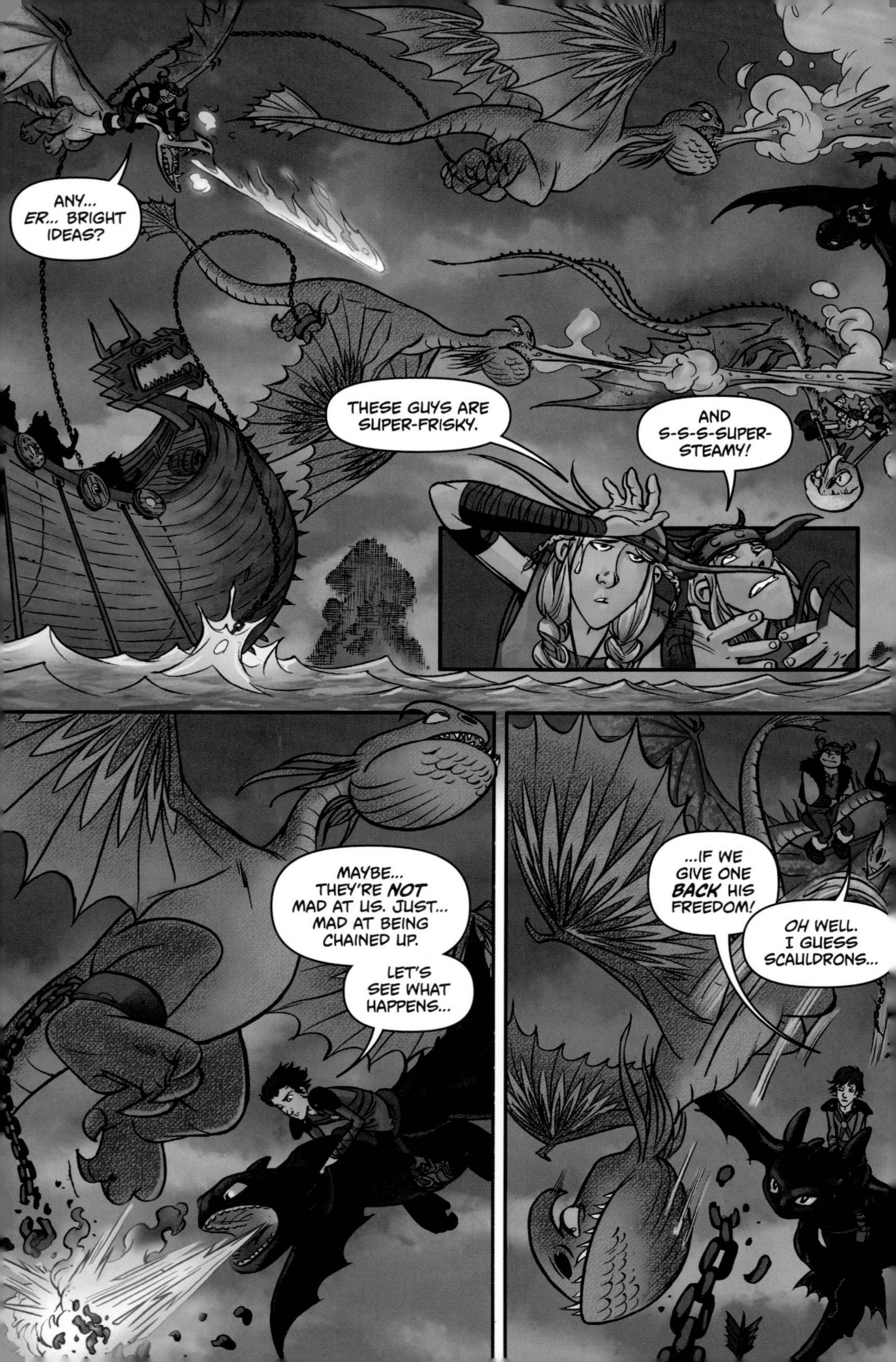
ANY... ER... BRIGHT IDEAS?
THESE GUYS ARE SUPER-FRISKY.
AND S-S-S-SUPER-STEAMY!
MAYBE... THEY'RE NOT MAD AT US. JUST... MAD AT BEING CHAINED UP.
LET'S SEE WHAT HAPPENS...
OH WELL. I GUESS SCAULDRONS...
...IF WE GIVE ONE BACK HIS FREEDOM!

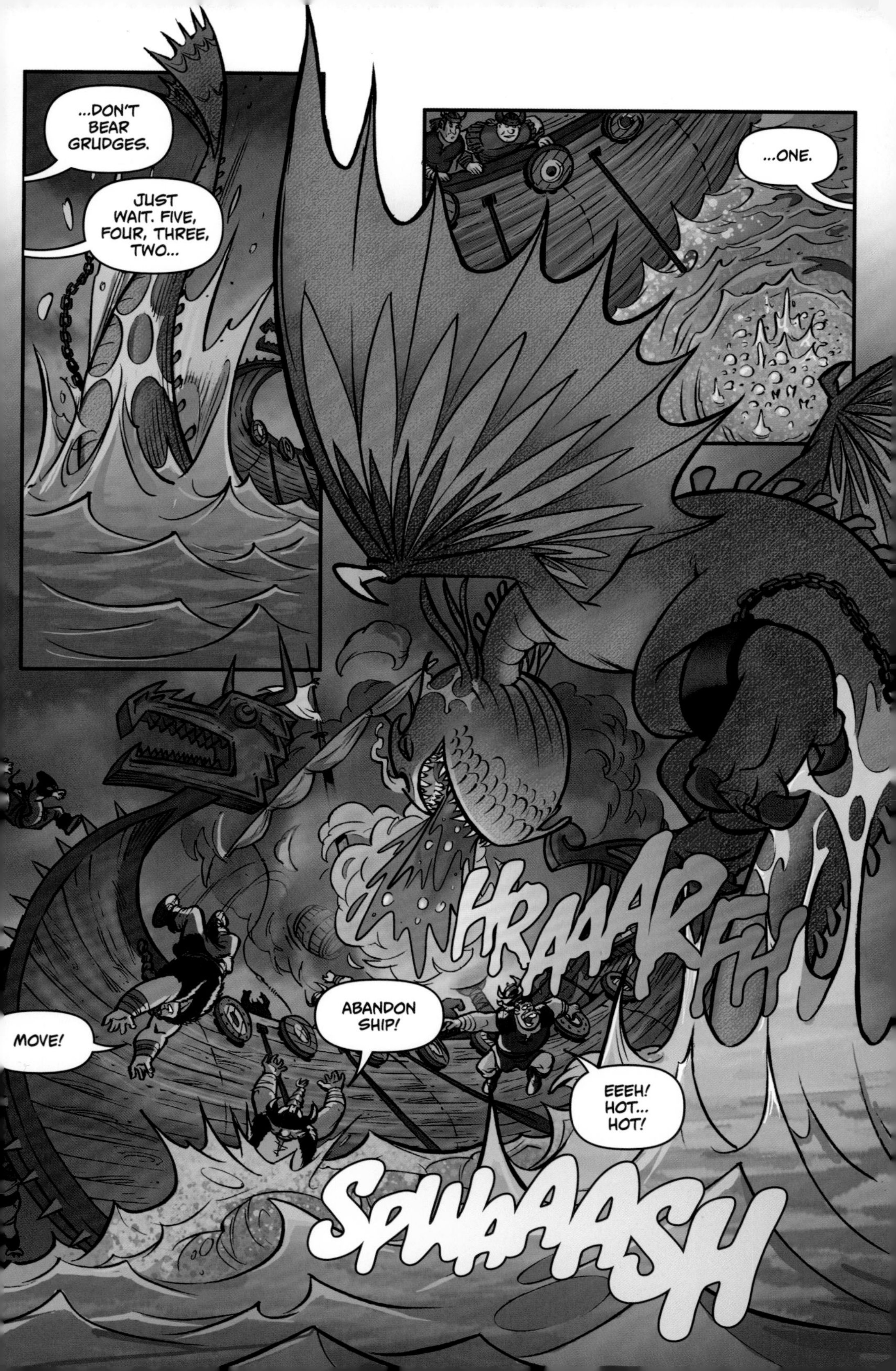
...DON'T BEAR GRUDGES.
JUST WAIT. FIVE, FOUR, THREE, TWO...
...ONE.
HRAAARRGH
MOVE!
ABANDON SHIP!
EEEH! HOT... HOT!
SPLUAAASH

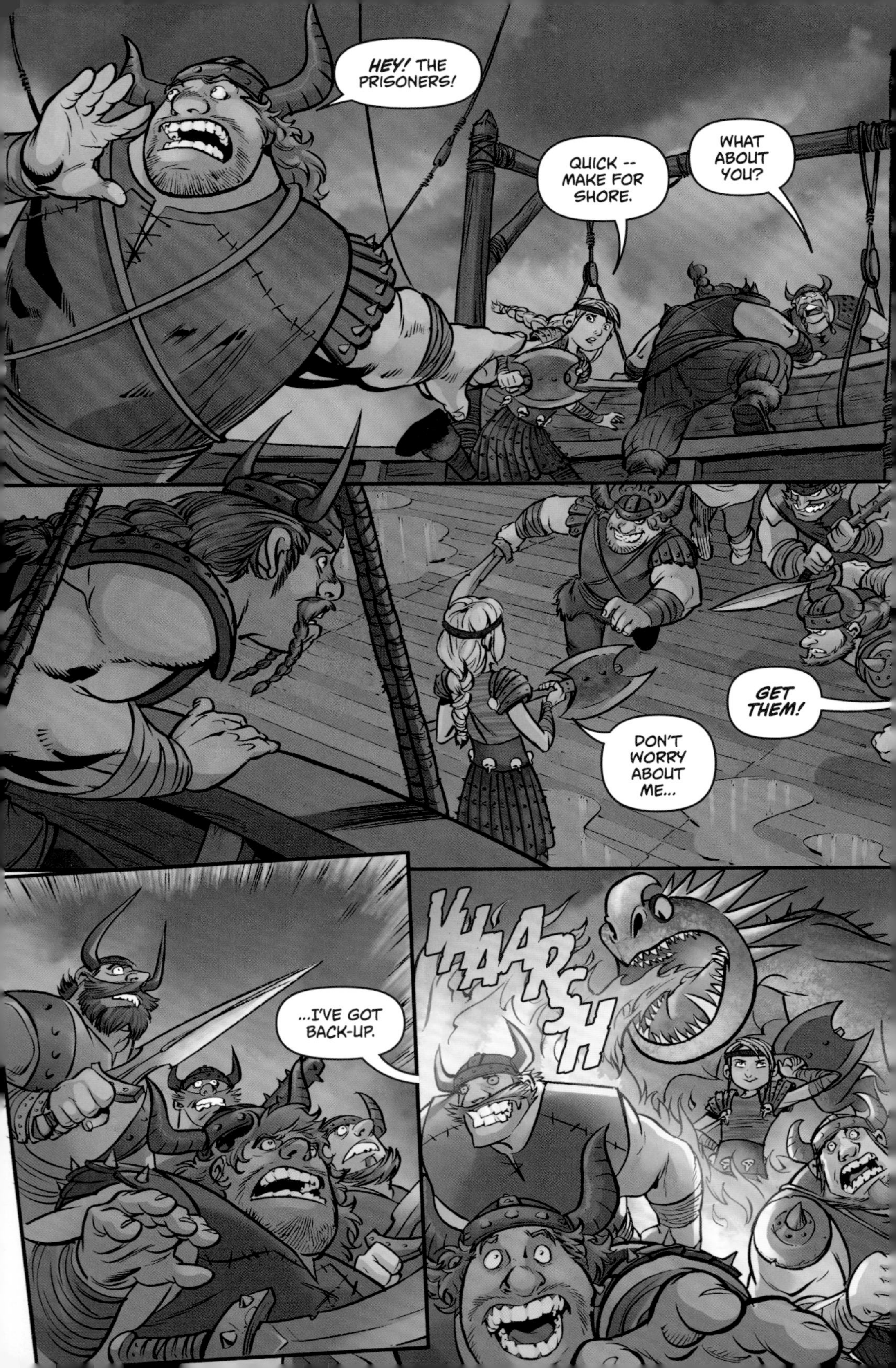
HEY! THE PRISONERS!
QUICK -- MAKE FOR SHORE.
WHAT ABOUT YOU?
GET THEM!
DON'T WORRY ABOUT ME...
...I'VE GOT BACK-UP.
YAARGH

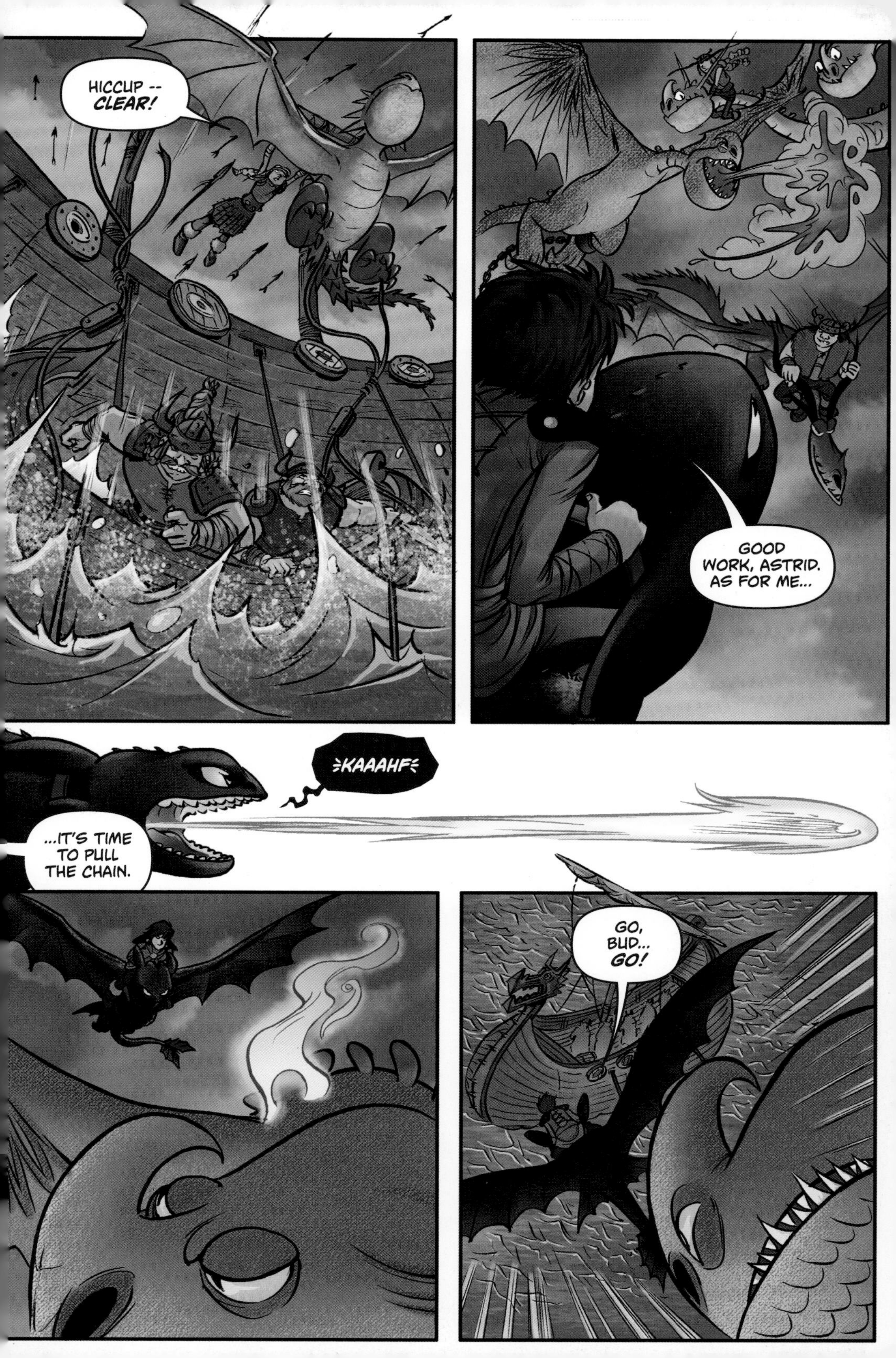
HICCUP -- CLEAR!
GOOD WORK, ASTRID. AS FOR ME...
KAAAHF
...IT'S TIME TO PULL THE CHAIN.
GO, BUD... GO!

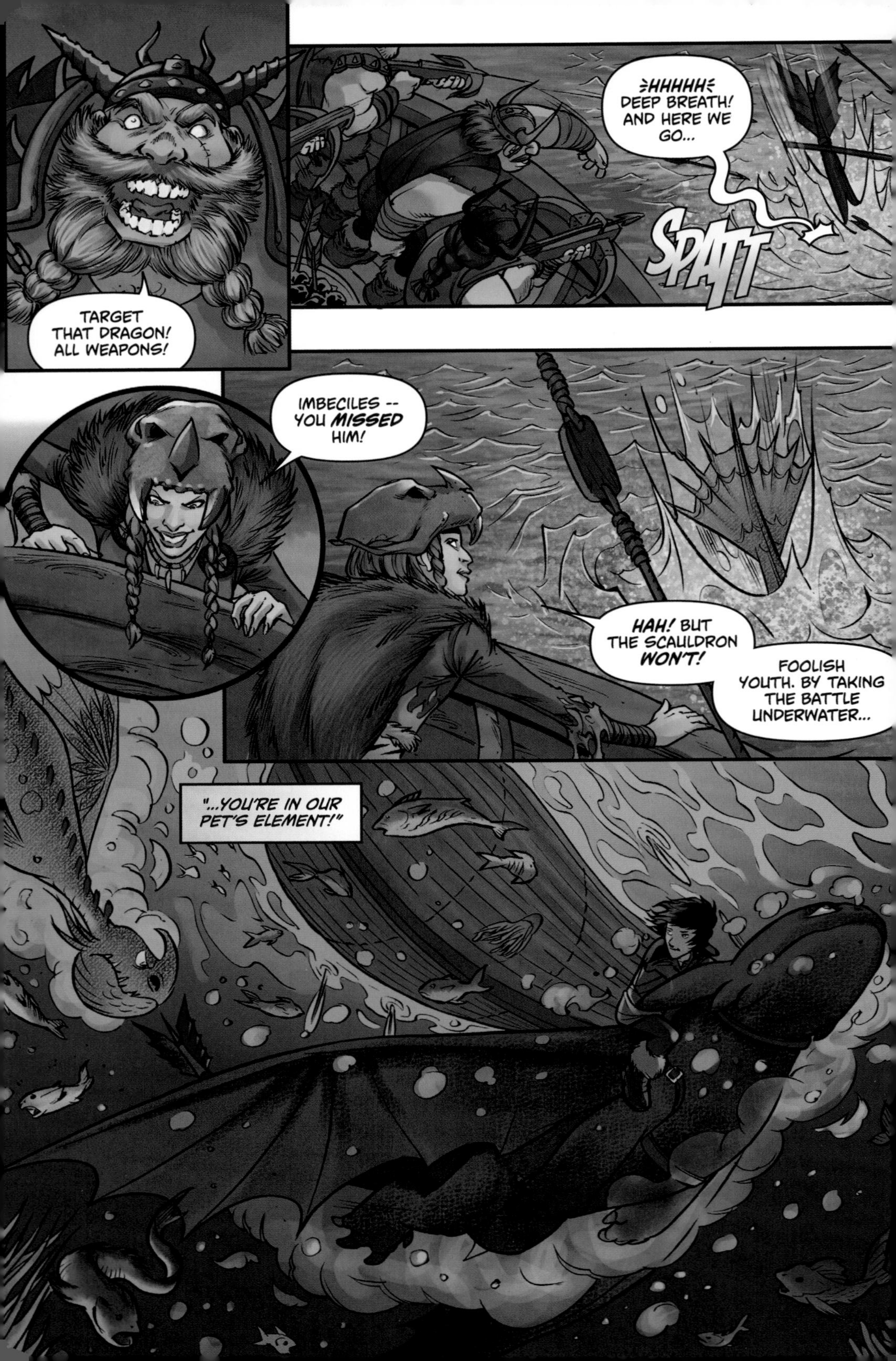
TARGET THAT DRAGON! ALL WEAPONS!
HHHHHH DEEP BREATH! AND HERE WE GO...
SPATT
IMBECILES -- YOU MISSED HIM!
HAH! BUT THE SCAULDRON WON'T!
FOOLISH YOUTH. BY TAKING THE BATTLE UNDERWATER...
"...YOU'RE IN OUR PET'S ELEMENT!"

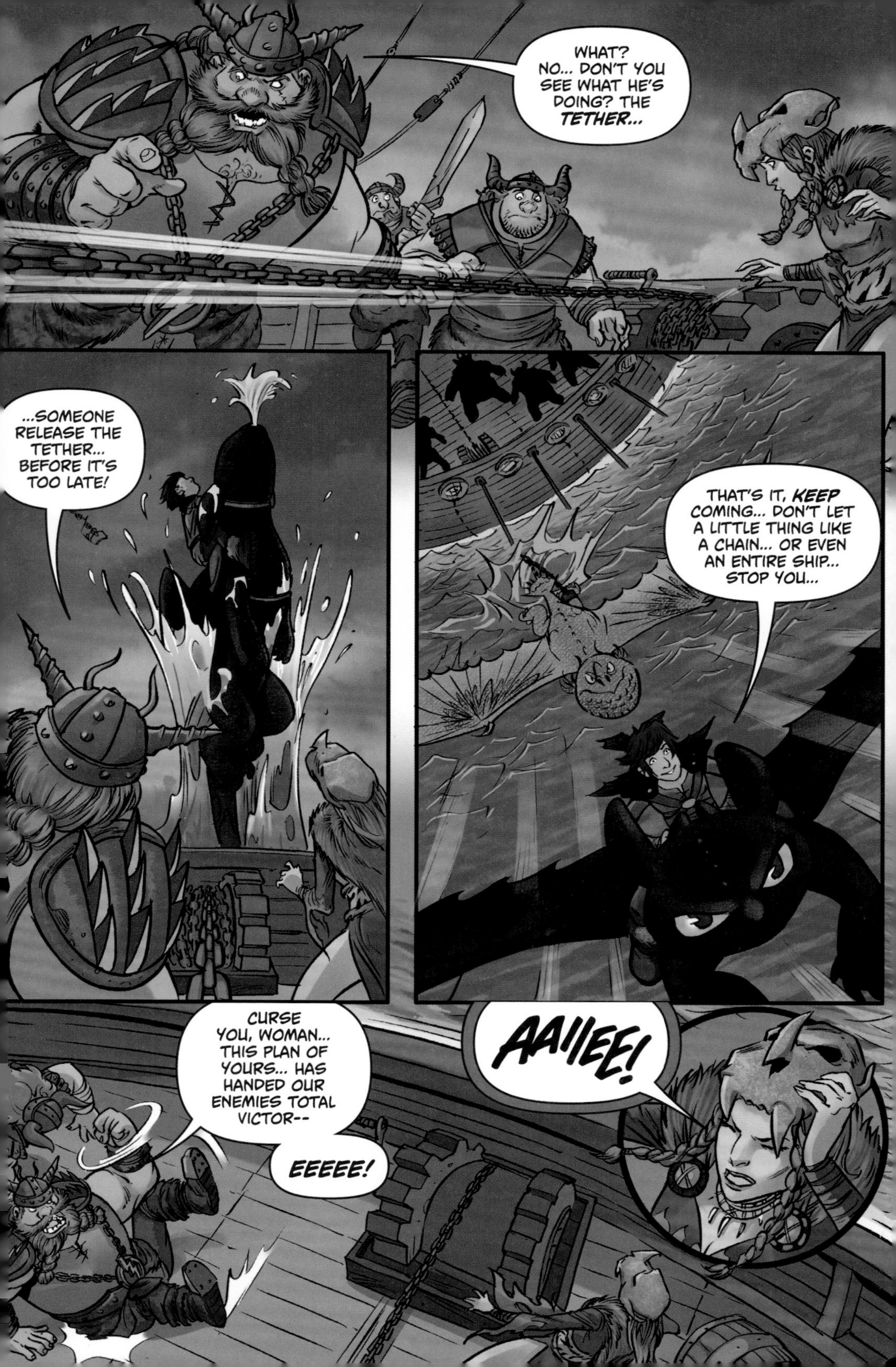
WHAT? NO... DON'T YOU SEE WHAT HE'S DOING? THE *TETHER*...
...SOMEONE RELEASE THE TETHER... BEFORE IT'S TOO LATE!
THAT'S IT, *KEEP* COMING... DON'T LET A LITTLE THING LIKE A CHAIN... OR EVEN AN ENTIRE SHIP... STOP YOU...
CURSE YOU, WOMAN... THIS PLAN OF YOURS... HAS HANDED OUR ENEMIES TOTAL VICTOR--
EEEEE!
AAIIEE!

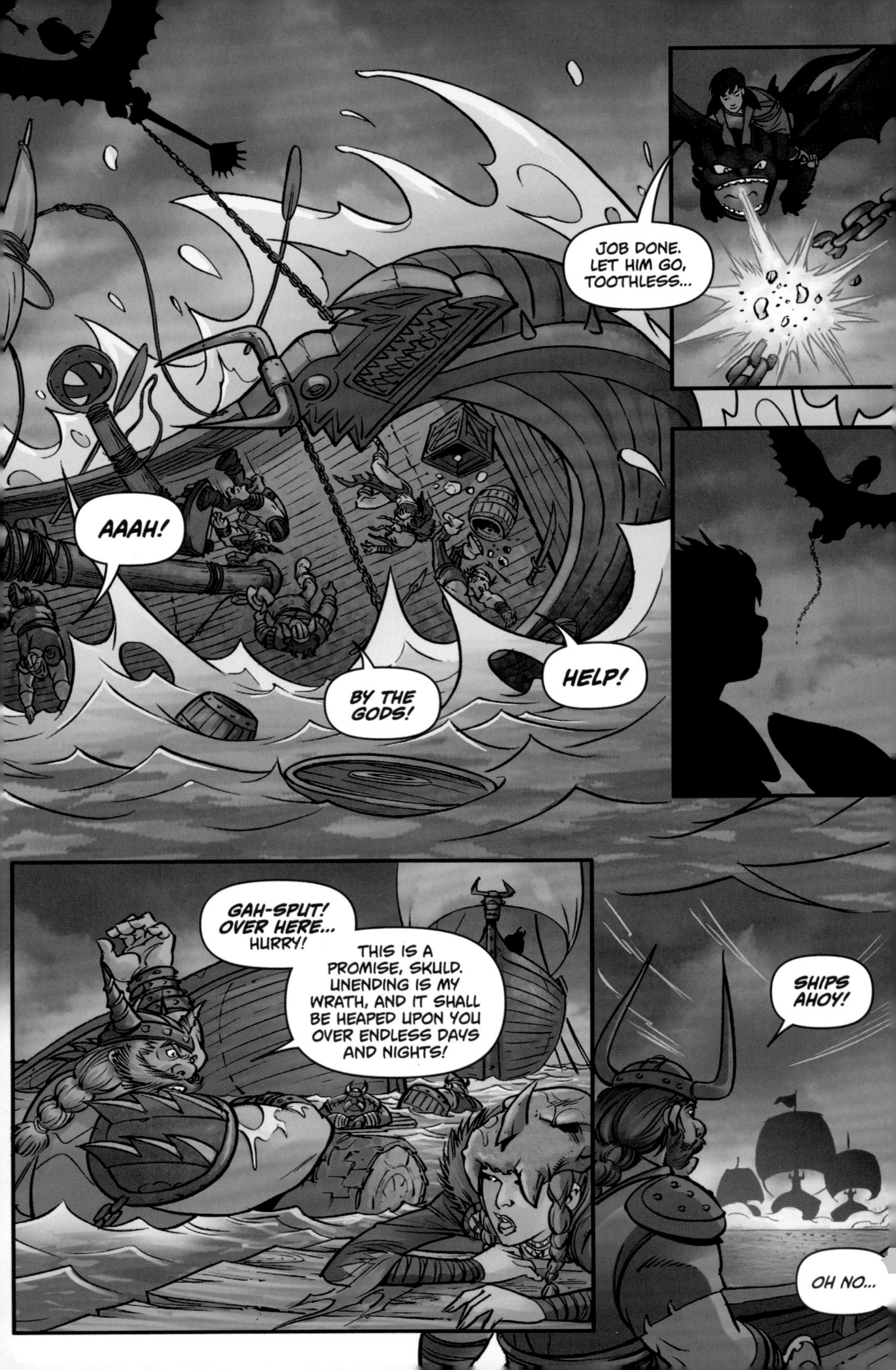
JOB DONE. LET HIM GO, TOOTHLESS...
AAAH!
BY THE GODS!
HELP!
GAH-SPUT! OVER HERE... HURRY!
THIS IS A PROMISE, SKULD. UNENDING IS MY WRATH, AND IT SHALL BE HEAPED UPON YOU OVER ENDLESS DAYS AND NIGHTS!
SHIPS AHOY!
OH NO...

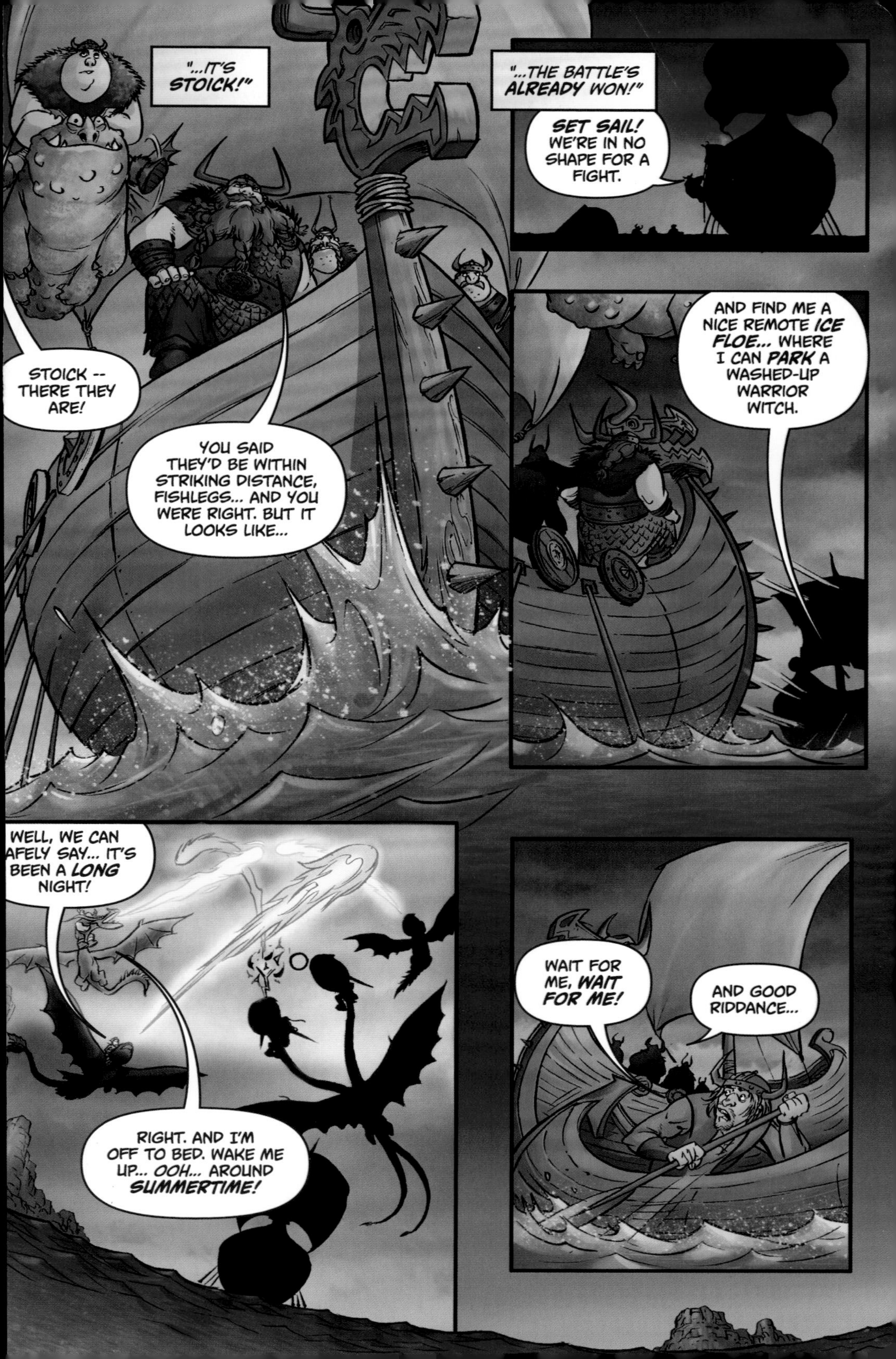

"...IT'S STOICK!"
STOICK -- THERE THEY ARE!
YOU SAID THEY'D BE WITHIN STRIKING DISTANCE, FISHLEGS... AND YOU WERE RIGHT. BUT IT LOOKS LIKE...
"...THE BATTLE'S ALREADY WON!"
SET SAIL! WE'RE IN NO SHAPE FOR A FIGHT.
AND FIND ME A NICE REMOTE ICE FLOE... WHERE I CAN PARK A WASHED-UP WARRIOR WITCH.
WELL, WE CAN AFELY SAY... IT'S BEEN A LONG NIGHT!
RIGHT. AND I'M OFF TO BED. WAKE ME UP... OOH... AROUND SUMMERTIME!
WAIT FOR ME, WAIT FOR ME!
AND GOOD RIDDANCE...

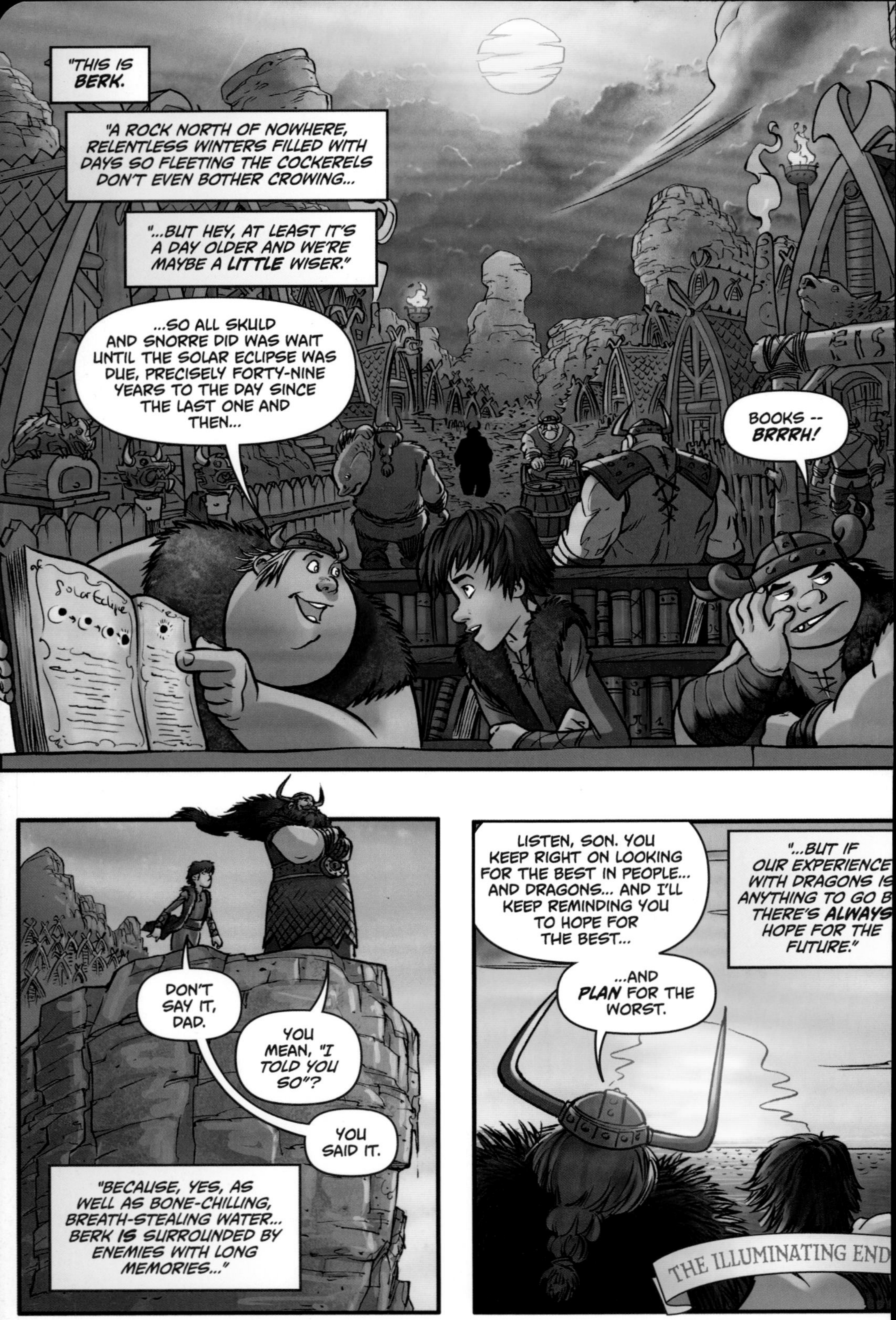
"THIS IS BERK.
"A ROCK NORTH OF NOWHERE, RELENTLESS WINTERS FILLED WITH DAYS SO FLEETING THE COCKERELS DON'T EVEN BOTHER CROWING...
"...BUT HEY, AT LEAST IT'S A DAY OLDER AND WE'RE MAYBE A LITTLE WISER."
...SO ALL SKULD AND SNORRE DID WAS WAIT UNTIL THE SOLAR ECLIPSE WAS DUE, PRECISELY FORTY-NINE YEARS TO THE DAY SINCE THE LAST ONE AND THEN...
BOOKS -- BRRRH!
Solar Eclipse
DON'T SAY IT, DAD.
YOU MEAN, "I TOLD YOU SO"?
YOU SAID IT.
"BECAUSE, YES, AS WELL AS BONE-CHILLING, BREATH-STEALING WATER... BERK IS SURROUNDED BY ENEMIES WITH LONG MEMORIES..."
LISTEN, SON. YOU KEEP RIGHT ON LOOKING FOR THE BEST IN PEOPLE... AND DRAGONS... AND I'LL KEEP REMINDING YOU TO HOPE FOR THE BEST...
...AND PLAN FOR THE WORST.
"...BUT IF OUR EXPERIENCE WITH DRAGONS IS ANYTHING TO GO B THERE'S ALWAYS HOPE FOR THE FUTURE."
THE ILLUMINATING END

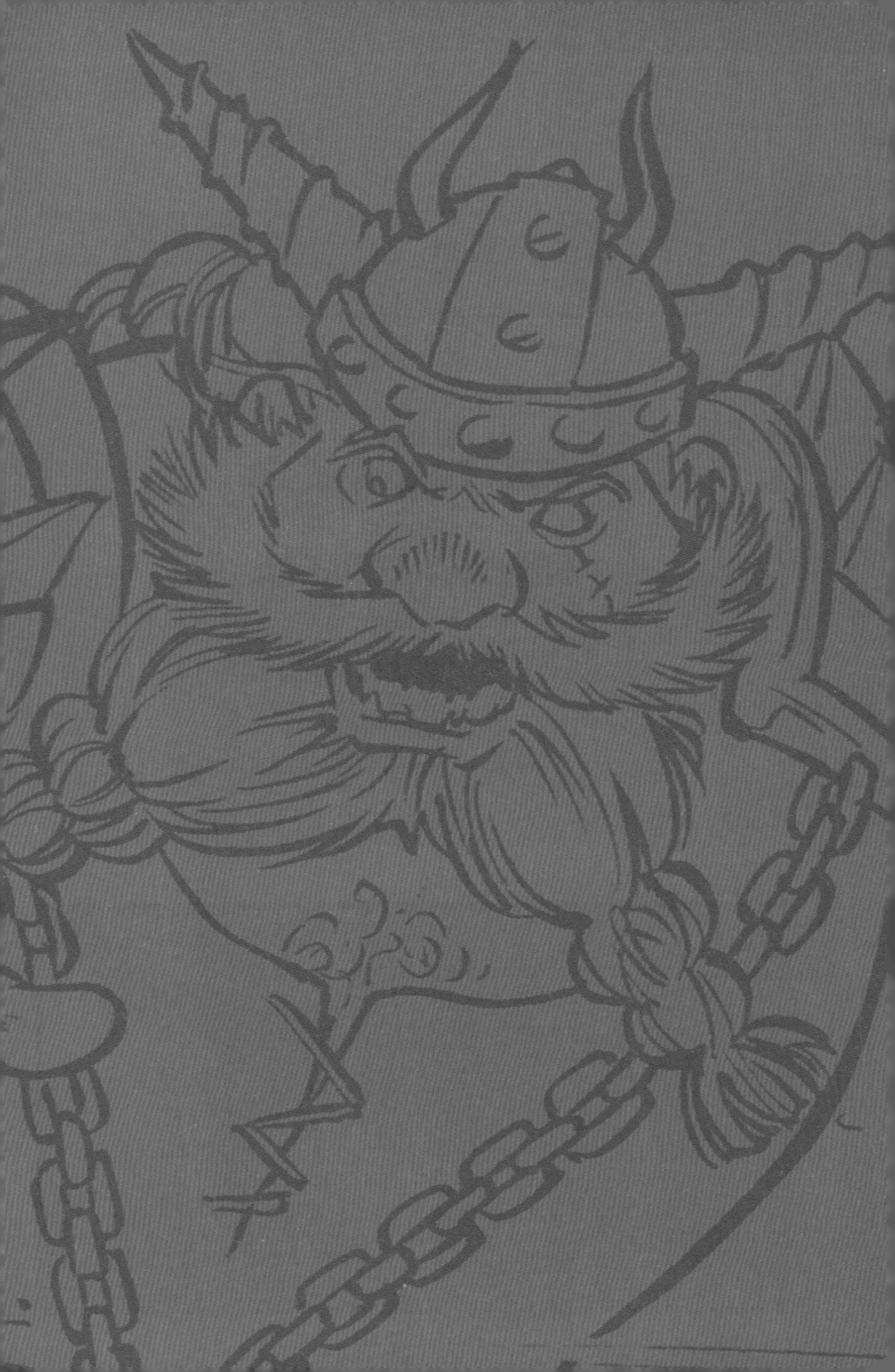

CRUEL TO BE KIND

SCRIPT
PAUL GOODENOUGH

PENCILS
ARIANNA FLOREAN

COLORS
CLAUDIA IANNICIELLO

LETTERING
JIM CAMPBELL

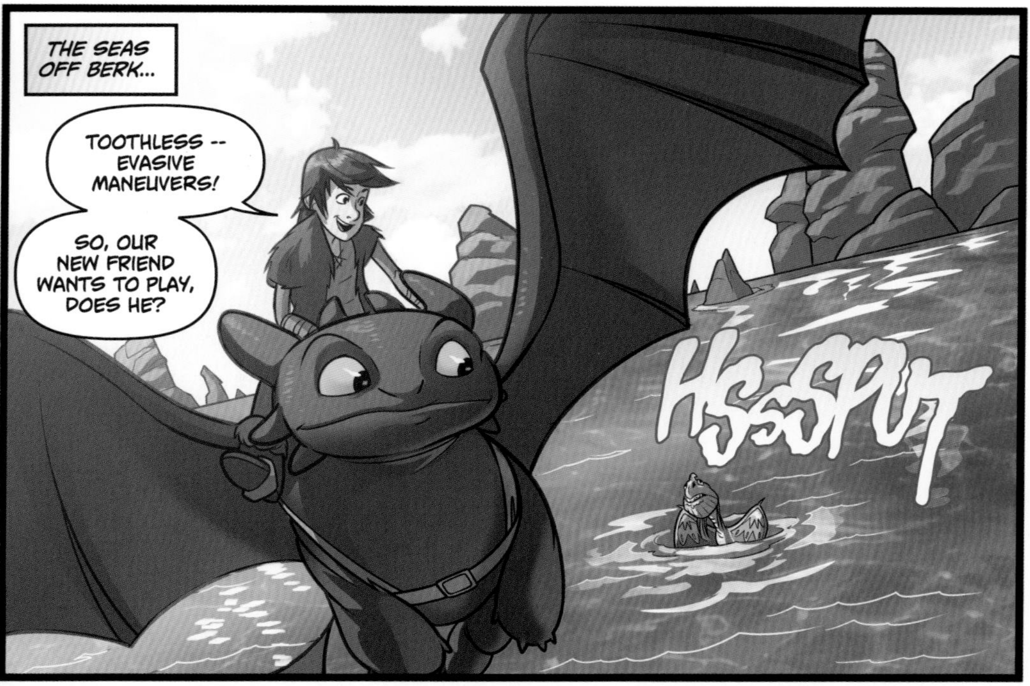
THE SEAS OFF BERK...
TOOTHLESS -- EVASIVE MANEUVERS!
SO, OUR NEW FRIEND WANTS TO PLAY, DOES HE?
HSSSPUT

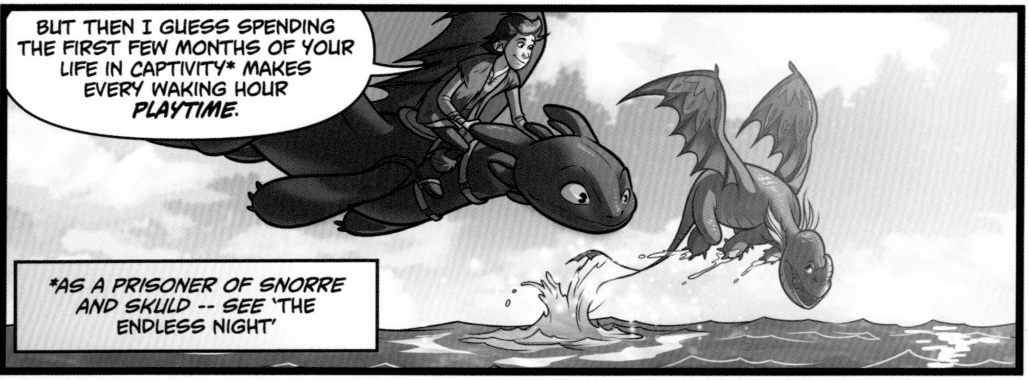
BUT THEN I GUESS SPENDING THE FIRST FEW MONTHS OF YOUR LIFE IN CAPTIVITY* MAKES EVERY WAKING HOUR PLAYTIME.
*AS A PRISONER OF SNORRE AND SKULD -- SEE 'THE ENDLESS NIGHT'

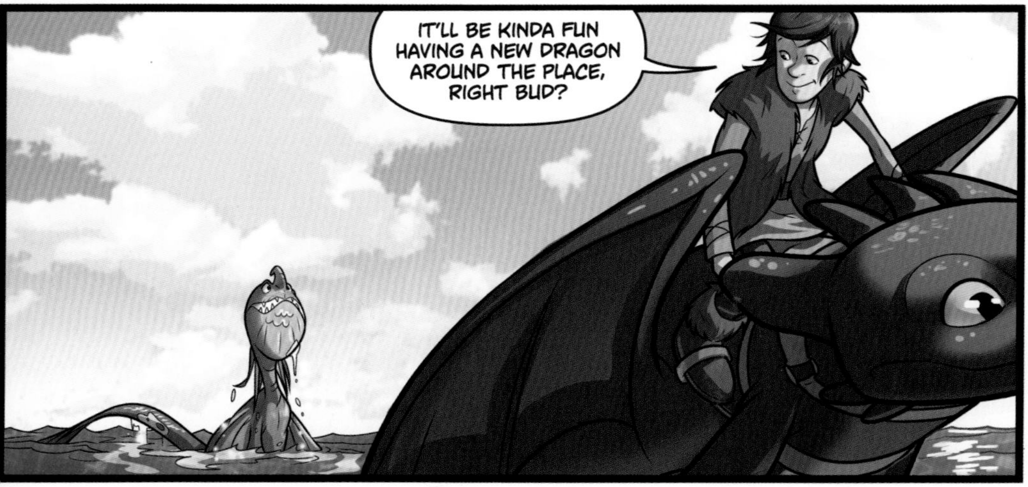
IT'LL BE KINDA FUN HAVING A NEW DRAGON AROUND THE PLACE, RIGHT BUD?

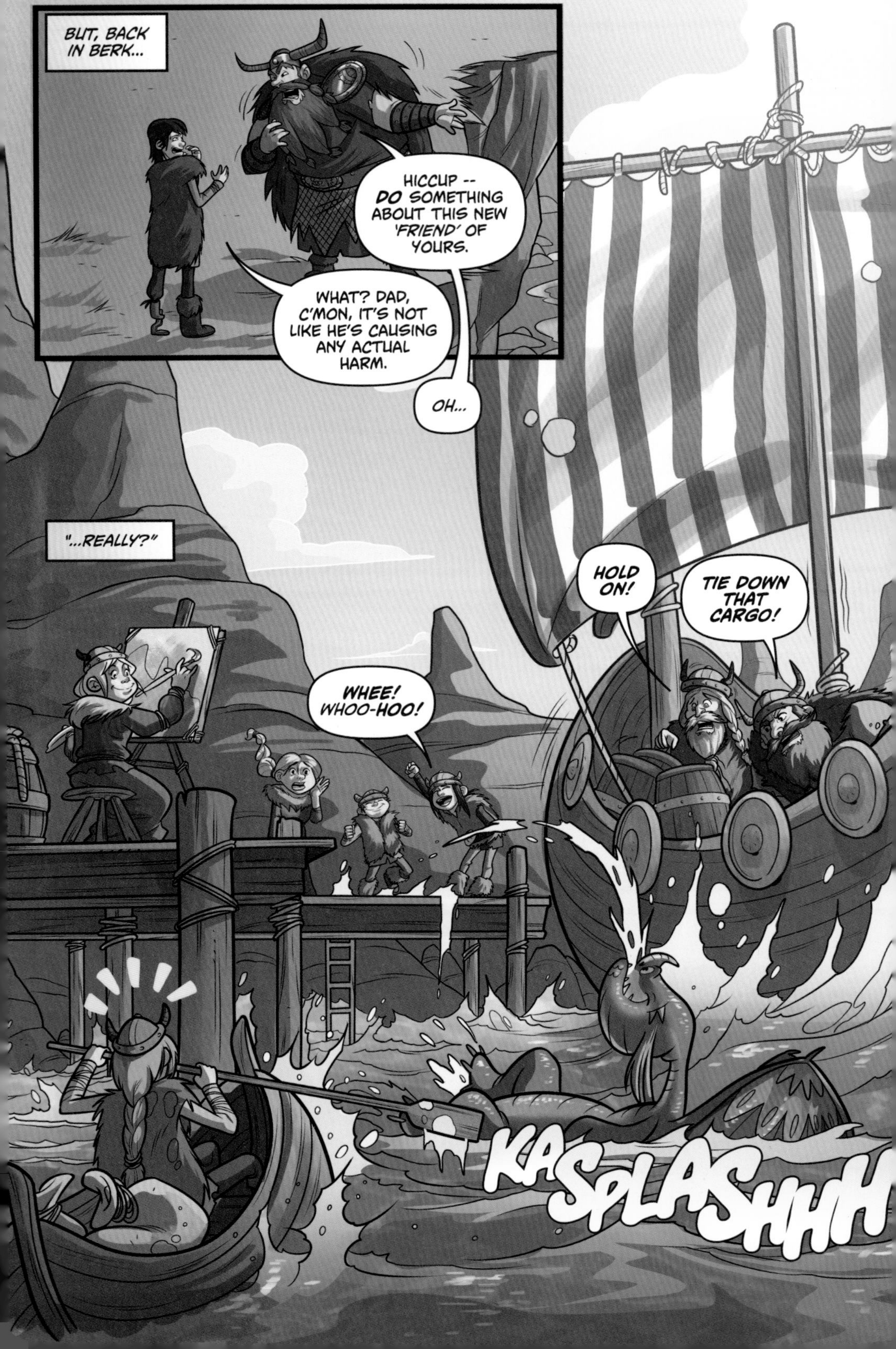

BUT, BACK IN BERK...
HICCUP -- DO SOMETHING ABOUT THIS NEW 'FRIEND' OF YOURS.
WHAT? DAD, C'MON, IT'S NOT LIKE HE'S CAUSING ANY ACTUAL HARM.
OH...
"...REALLY?"
HOLD ON!
TIE DOWN THAT CARGO!
WHEE! WHOO-HOO!
KASPLASHHH

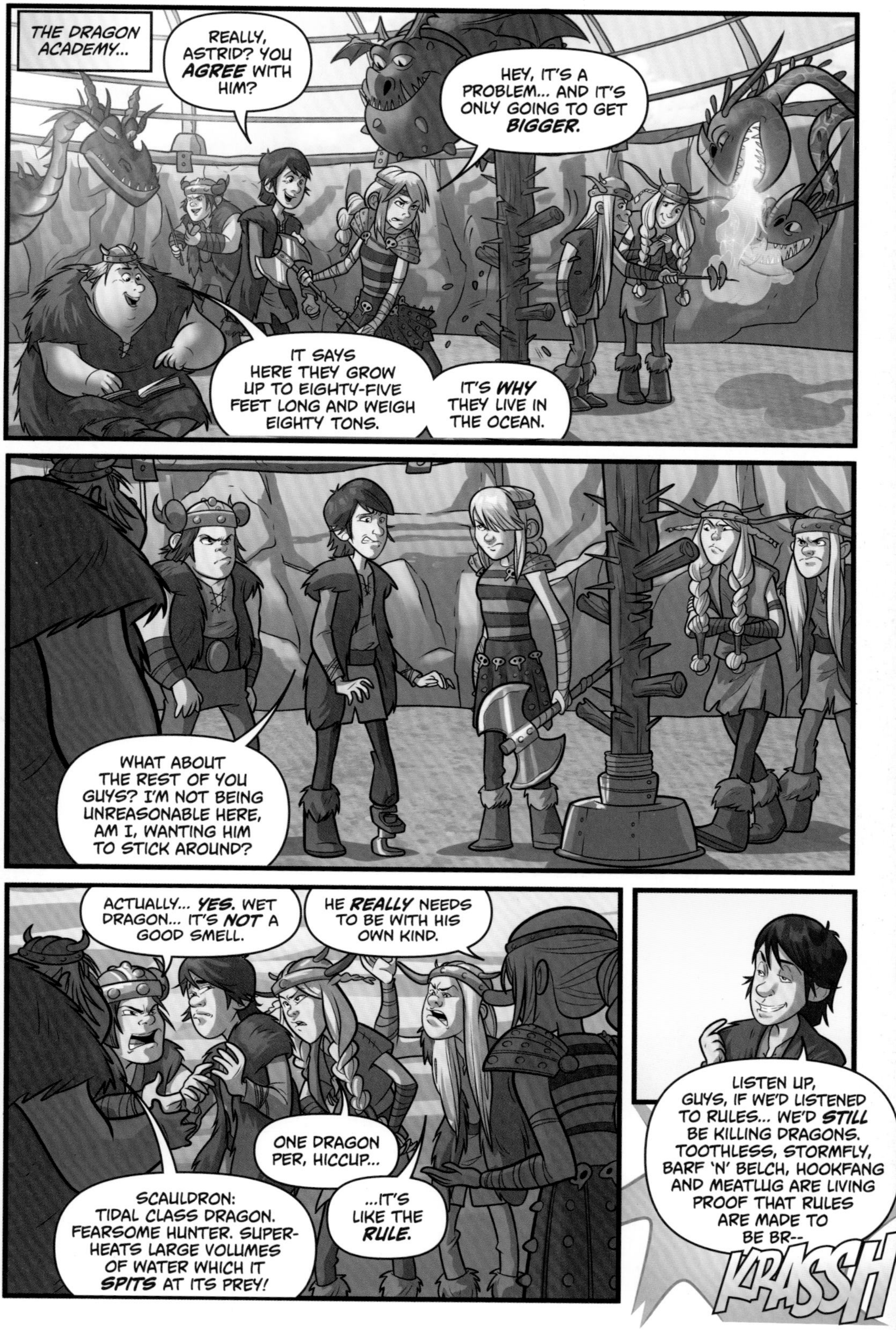
THE DRAGON ACADEMY...
REALLY, ASTRID? YOU AGREE WITH HIM?
HEY, IT'S A PROBLEM... AND IT'S ONLY GOING TO GET BIGGER.
IT SAYS HERE THEY GROW UP TO EIGHTY-FIVE FEET LONG AND WEIGH EIGHTY TONS.
IT'S WHY THEY LIVE IN THE OCEAN.
WHAT ABOUT THE REST OF YOU GUYS? I'M NOT BEING UNREASONABLE HERE, AM I, WANTING HIM TO STICK AROUND?
ACTUALLY... YES. WET DRAGON... IT'S NOT A GOOD SMELL.
HE REALLY NEEDS TO BE WITH HIS OWN KIND.
ONE DRAGON PER, HICCUP...
...IT'S LIKE THE RULE.
SCAULDRON: TIDAL CLASS DRAGON. FEARSOME HUNTER. SUPER-HEATS LARGE VOLUMES OF WATER WHICH IT SPITS AT ITS PREY!
LISTEN UP, GUYS, IF WE'D LISTENED TO RULES... WE'D STILL BE KILLING DRAGONS. TOOTHLESS, STORMFLY, BARF 'N' BELCH, HOOKFANG AND MEATLUG ARE LIVING PROOF THAT RULES ARE MADE TO BE BR--
KRASSH

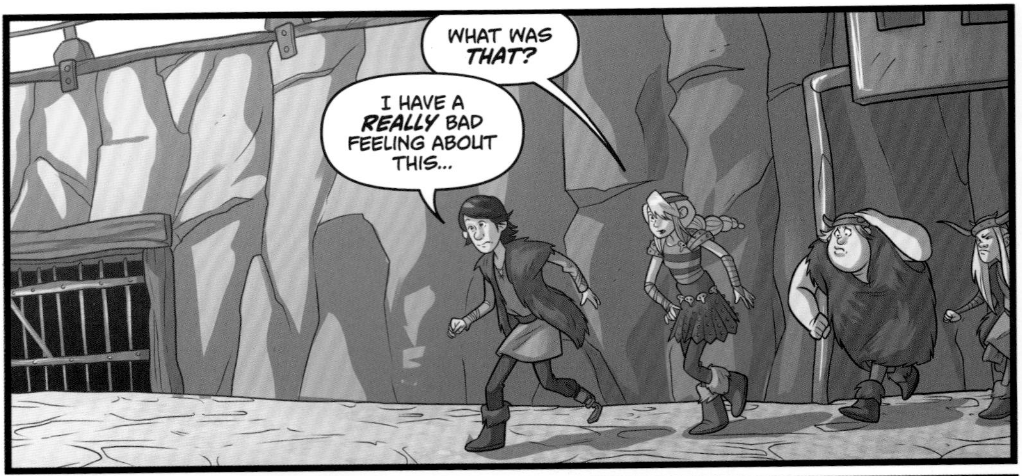
WHAT WAS *THAT?*
I HAVE A *REALLY* BAD FEELING ABOUT THIS...

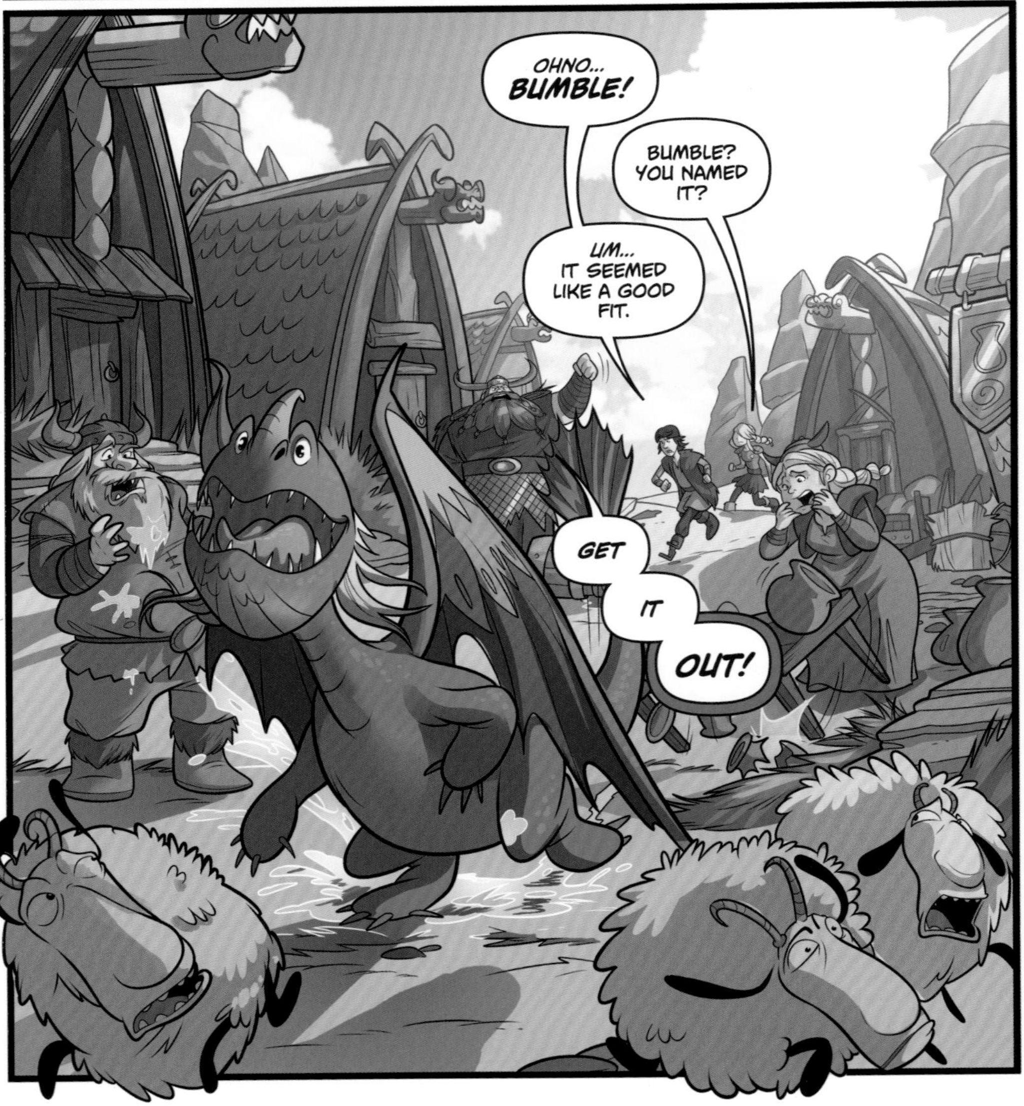
OHNO... **BUMBLE!**
BUMBLE? YOU NAMED IT?
UM... IT SEEMED LIKE A GOOD FIT.
GET
IT
OUT!

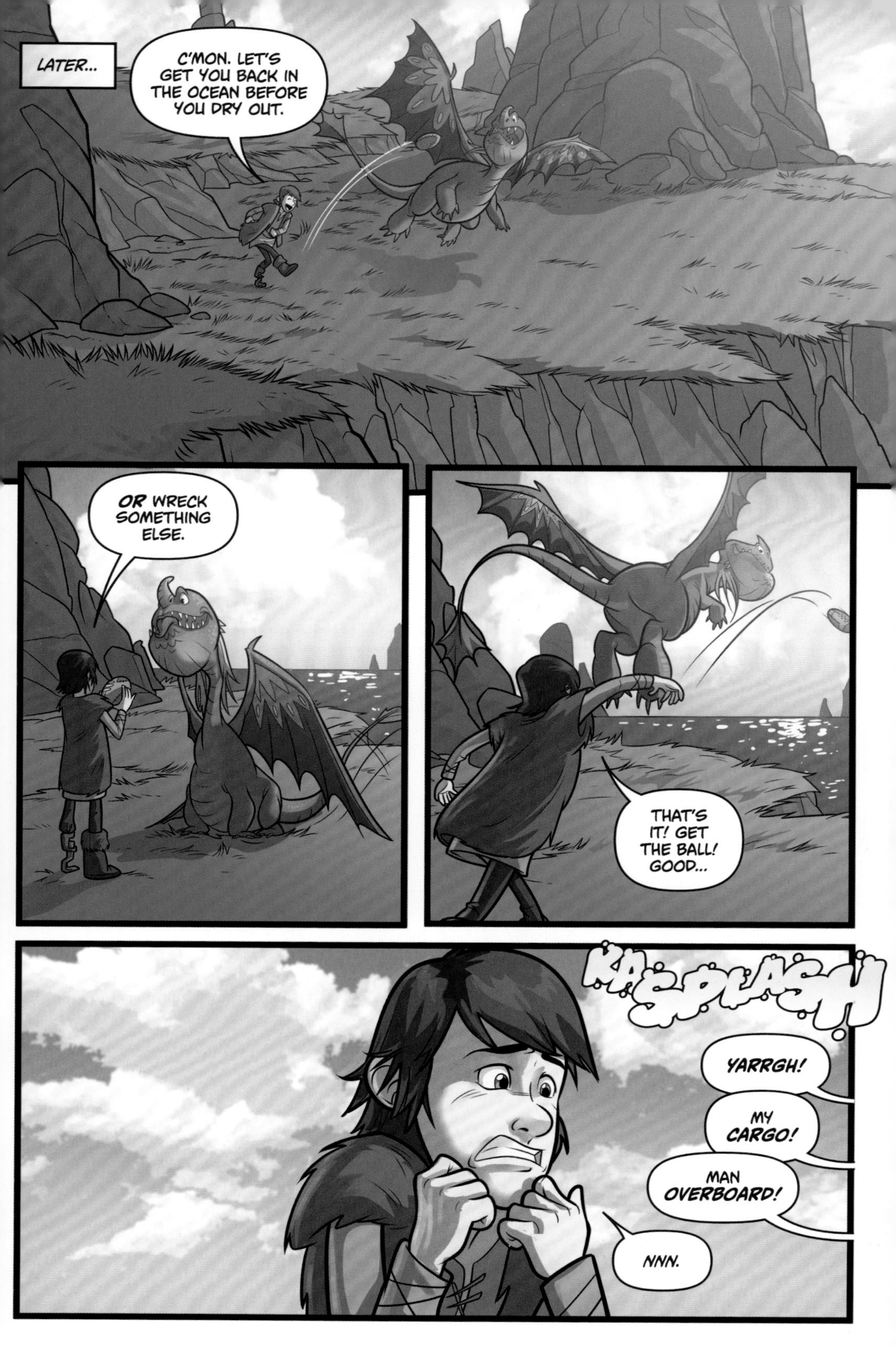
LATER...
C'MON. LET'S GET YOU BACK IN THE OCEAN BEFORE YOU DRY OUT.
OR WRECK SOMETHING ELSE.
THAT'S IT! GET THE BALL! GOOD...
KA-SPLASH!
YARRGH!
MY CARGO!
MAN OVERBOARD!
NNN.

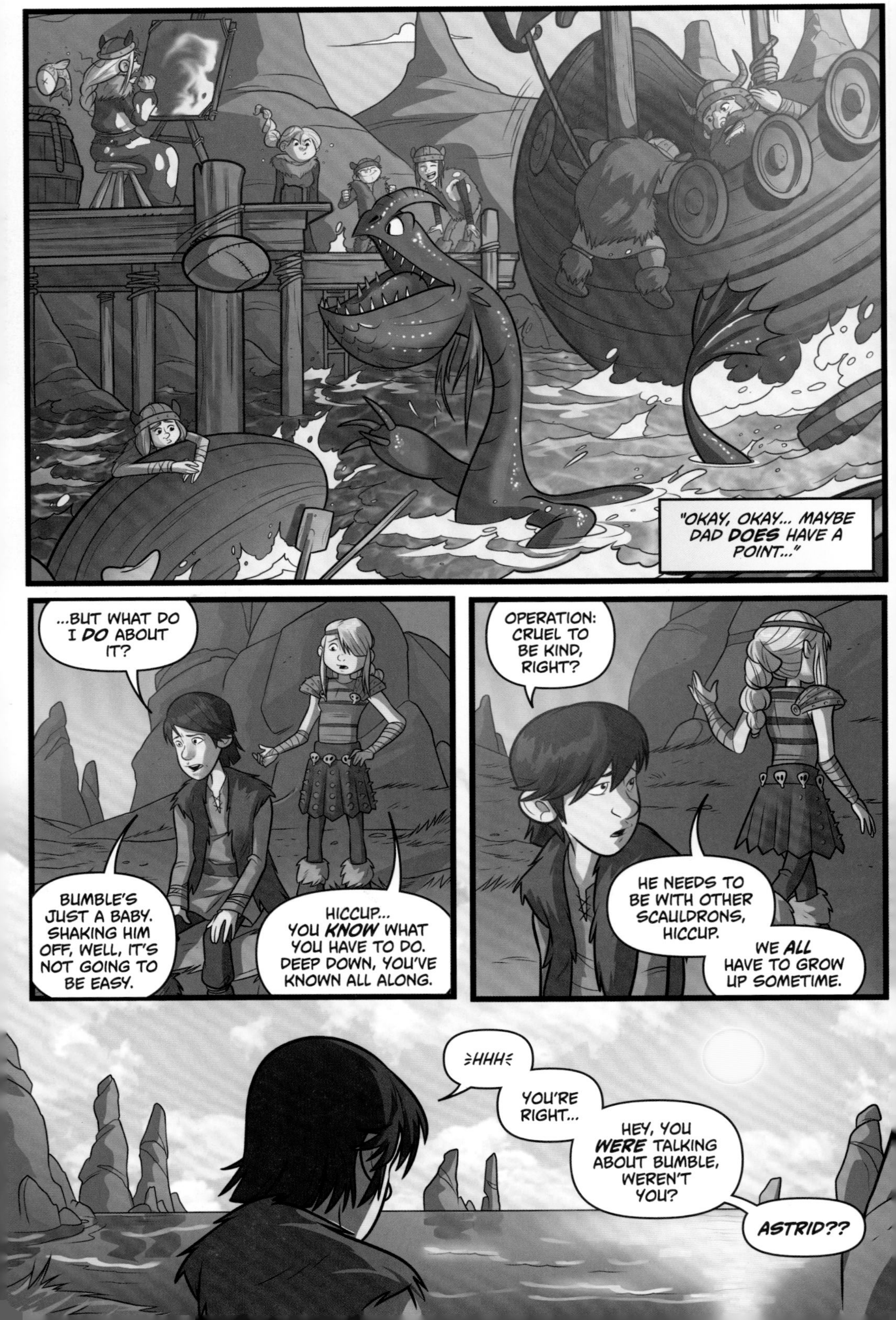
"OKAY, OKAY... MAYBE DAD DOES HAVE A POINT..."
...BUT WHAT DO I DO ABOUT IT?
BUMBLE'S JUST A BABY. SHAKING HIM OFF, WELL, IT'S NOT GOING TO BE EASY.
HICCUP... YOU KNOW WHAT YOU HAVE TO DO. DEEP DOWN, YOU'VE KNOWN ALL ALONG.
OPERATION: CRUEL TO BE KIND, RIGHT?
HE NEEDS TO BE WITH OTHER SCAULDRONS, HICCUP.
WE ALL HAVE TO GROW UP SOMETIME.
HHH
YOU'RE RIGHT...
HEY, YOU WERE TALKING ABOUT BUMBLE, WEREN'T YOU?
ASTRID??

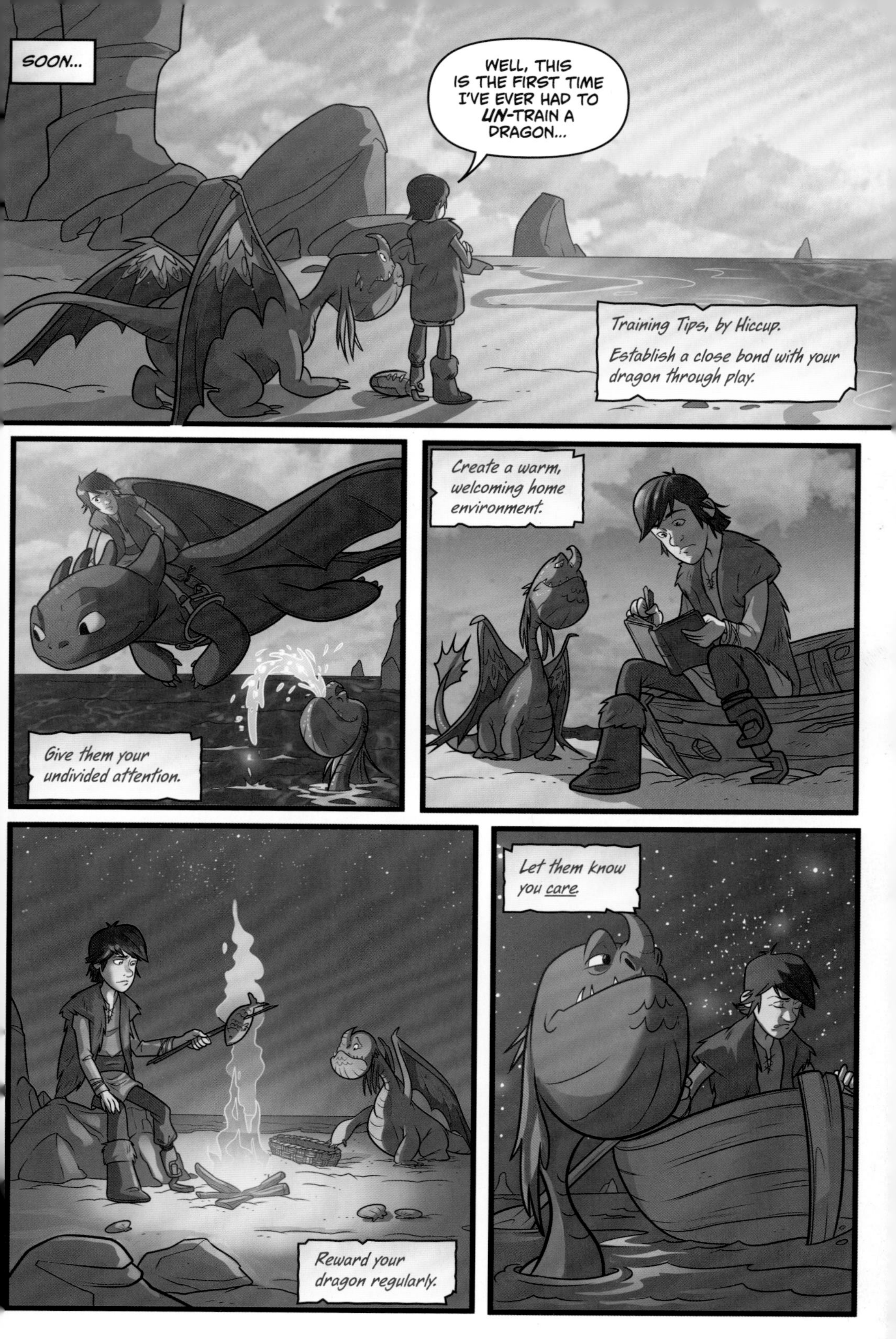
SOON...
WELL, THIS IS THE FIRST TIME I'VE EVER HAD TO UN-TRAIN A DRAGON...
Training Tips, by Hiccup.
Establish a close bond with your dragon through play.
Give them your undivided attention.
Create a warm, welcoming home environment.
Reward your dragon regularly.
Let them know you care.

SOON...

NOT TOO FAST, BUD... WE DON'T WANT TO LOSE HIM.

AHA -- THERE'S ASTRID. I GUESS SHE *FOUND* WHAT WE'RE LOOKING FOR...

...A *POD* OF SCAULDRONS!

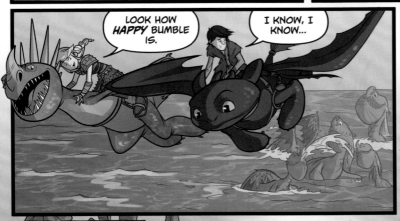

LOOK HOW *HAPPY* BUMBLE IS.

I KNOW, I KNOW...

Follow these simple steps and you'll have a friend for life.

"...HE'S PROBABLY ALREADY FORGOTTEN US."

THE BLUBBERING END